PENGUIN BOOKS

THIS BLINDING ABSENCE OF LIGHT

Winner of the 1994 Prix Maghreb, Tahar Ben Jelloun was born in 1944 in Fez, Morocco, and emigrated to France in 1961. A novelist, essayist, critic and poet, he is a regular contributor to *Le Monde*, *La Répubblica*, *El País* and *Panorama*. His novels include *The Sacred Night*, which received the Prix Goncourt in 1987 and *Corruption* (The New Press).

Linda Coverdale's most recent translation for The New Press is Marie Darrieussecq's *Undercurrents*. She won the French American Foundation's Translation Prize in 1997. She lives in Brooklyn, New York.

THIS BLINDING ABSENCE
OF LIGHT

TAHAR BEN JELLOUN

Translated by Linda Coverdale

PENGUIN BOOKS

PENGUIN BOOKS

Published by the Penguin Group
Penguin Books Ltd, 80 Strand, London WC2R 0RL, England
Penguin Group (USA) Inc., 375 Hudson Street, New York, New York 10014, USA
Penguin Group (Canada), 90 Eglinton Avenue East, Suite 700, Toronto, Ontario, Canada M4P 3YZ
(a division of Pearson Penguin Canada Inc.)
Penguin Ireland, 25 St Stephen's Green, Dublin 2, Ireland (a division of Penguin Books Ltd)
Penguin Group (Australia), 250 Camberwell Road, Camberwell, Victoria 3124, Australia
(a division of Pearson Australia Group Pty Ltd)
Penguin Books India Pvt Ltd, 11 Community Centre,
Panchsheel Park, New Delhi – 110 017, India
Penguin Group (NZ), cnr Airborne and Rosedale Roads, Albany,
Auckland 1310, New Zealand (a division of Pearson New Zealand Ltd)
Penguin Books (South Africa) (Pty) Ltd, 24 Sturdee Avenue, Rosebank 2196, Johannesburg, South Africa

Penguin Books Ltd, Registered Offices: 80 Strand, London WC2R 0RL, England

www.penguin.com

Cette aveuglante absence de lumière first published by Éditions du Seuil, 2001
Published in the United States by The New Press, New York, 2002
Published in Great Britain in Penguin Books 2005

6

Cette aveuglante absence de lumière copyright © Éditions du Seuil, 2001
English translation by Linda Coverdale © The New Press, 2002
All rights reserved

The moral right of the author has been asserted

Printed in England by Clays Ltd, St Ives plc

This novel is based upon real events drawn from the testimony of a former inmate of Tazmamart Prison. It is dedicated to Aziz and to Réda, his young son, light of his third life.

TRANSLATOR'S NOTE

An asterisk in the text signifies the first appearance of a term included in the glossary I have provided at the end of the book.

THIS BLINDING ABSENCE
OF LIGHT

For a long time I searched for the black stone that cleanses the soul of death. When I say a long time, I think of a bottomless pit, a tunnel dug with my fingers, my teeth, in the stubborn hope of glimpsing, if only for a minute, one infinitely lingering minute, a ray of light, a spark that would imprint itself deep within my eye, that would stay protected in my entrails like a secret. There it would be, lodging in my breast and nourishing my endless nights, there, in the depths of the humid earth, in that tomb smelling of man stripped of his humanity by shovel blows that flay him alive, snatching away his sight, his voice, and his reason.

But what good was reason there, in our graves? I mean where we had been laid in the earth, left with a hole so we could breathe, so we could live for enough time, for enough nights to pay for our mistake, left with death in the guise of a subtle slowness, a death that was to take its time, all the time men have—the men we were no longer, and those who still kept watch over us, and those who had completely forgotten us. Oh, slowness! It was the chief enemy, the one that enveloped our battered bodies, leaving our open wounds plenty of time before they began to scar over, this slowness that made our hearts beat to the peaceful rhythm of *la petite mort,* as though we were supposed to fade away, a candle flickering in the distance and burning itself out as calmly as happiness. I often thought about that candle, made not of wax but of some unknown substance that gave the illusion of an eternal flame, symbolic of our survival. And I used to think about a giant hourglass, in which each grain of sand was a speck of our skin, a drop of our blood, a tiny breath of oxygen lost to us as time descended toward the abyss where we lay.

But where were we? We had arrived there unable to see. Was it nighttime? Probably. Night would be our companion, our territory, our world, and our cemetery. That was the first thing I learned. My survival, my wretchedness, my agony were inscribed on the veil of night. I knew this right away. It was as if I had always known this. Ah, night! My blanket of frozen dust, my fingers crushed by the butt of an automatic pistol, my stand of black trees set shivering by an icy wind to make my legs ache.... Night did not fall, as the expression goes; night was there, everlastingly. Queen of our sufferings, she brought them to our attention, in case we had managed to stop feeling anything, the way some of us did by concentrating so intensely that we slipped free from our bodies, and thus from our pain. We abandoned our bodies to the torturers and went off to forget all that in prayer or in some secret corner of the heart.

Night clothed us. In another world, one would say that night waited on us hand and foot. Above all, no light. Never the slightest ray of light. But even though we had lost our sight, our eyes had adjusted to this. We saw in the dark, or thought we did. Our images were shadows shifting about in the gloom, bumping into one another, even knocking over the water jug, or moving the morsel of stale bread some of us saved to ward off stomach cramps.

Night was no longer night, since there were no more days, no more stars, no more moon, no more sky. We were the night. We had become nocturnal: our bodies, breathing, heartbeats, the fumbling of our hands moving effortlessly from one wall to another in a space shrunk to the dimensions of a tomb for the living, although whenever I say that word, I should use "surviving" instead, yet I really was a living being, enduring life in extreme deprivation, an ordeal that could end only in death but that seemed strangely like life.

We were not in just any night. Ours was dank, very dank, sticky, dirty, clammy, smelling of human and rat urine, a night that came to us on a gray horse followed by a pack of mad dogs. Night had thrown her cloak over our faces no longer astonished by anything, a cloak without even the tiniest moth holes, oh, no: it was a cloak of wet sand. Earth mixed with the excrement of all kinds of animals settled on our skin, as though our funeral were over. The wind blowing in the cloak did bring us a little air so we would not die right away, just enough air to keep us far from life and quite close to death. This cloak weighed tons. Invisible and yet tangible. My fingers were rubbed raw when I touched it. I hid my hands behind my back to avoid all contact with the night, protecting them like that, but many a time I was forced by the chill of the damp cement to change positions, to lie prone, face pressed against the floor, preferring an aching forehead to aching hands. So there were preferences between two pains. Well, not really. The entire body had to suffer, every part, without exception. The tomb was arranged (another of life's words, but one does have to keep borrowing little things from life) so that the body would experience all imaginable torments, endure them ever so slowly, and remain alive to undergo further agony.

Actually, the tomb was a cell just under ten feet long and half as wide. Most of all, it was low, only about five feet high. I could not stand up. There was a hole for pissing and crapping. A hole less than four inches in diameter. The hole was a part of our bodies. We had to forget our existence fast, stop smelling the shit and urine, stop smelling anything at all. We couldn't very well hold our noses, no, we had to keep them open without smelling a single thing. That was difficult, at first. It was an apprenticeship, a necessary madness, a test we absolutely had to pass. Being there without being there. Shutting down my five senses, directing them elsewhere, giving them another life, as though I had been thrown into that grave without them. That's what it was—acting as though I had left them at a baggage checkroom, tucked away in a small suitcase, carefully wrapped in cotton or silk, then set aside without the torturers' knowledge, without anyone's knowledge. Betting on the future.

I fell into the pit like a bag of sand, like a package that looked human, I fell and I experienced nothing, I felt nothing and did not hurt anywhere. No: that state—I reached it only after years of suffering. I even believe the pain helped me. Through misery, through anguish, I slowly managed to withdraw from my body and see myself fighting the scorpion in that grave. I was hovering overhead. I was on the other side of night. But before I got there, I had to trudge for centuries through the darkness of a tunnel without end.

We had no beds, not even a piece of foam rubber for a mattress, not even a bale of hay or the esparto grass* that animals sleep on. Each of us received two gray blankets bearing the printed number 1936. Was it the year of their manufacture or a specific code for those condemned to a slow death? Sturdy and light, the blankets had a hospital smell. They must have been soaked in disinfectant. We had to get used to it. In the summer they were not really necessary, while in the winter they were inadequate. I folded one to make a very narrow mattress. I slept on my side. When I wanted to change sides, I got up so as not to undo the folds. And like clockwork, especially in the beginning, I hit my head against the ceiling.

I wrapped myself in the other blanket and breathed the disinfectant, which gave me strange headaches. They were poisoned blankets!

How many times did I convince myself that the earth was going to gape open and swallow me! Everything had been quite well planned. For instance, we were allowed five quarts of water a day. Who had specified this amount? Doctors, probably. Anyway, the water was not really drinkable. I would pour some into a plastic jug I had and let it sit for a whole day. At the bottom of the jug would be a deposit of silt and slimy filth.

Since they had provided for everything, perhaps they had laid the flooring in the cell so that it would tilt after a few months or years and hurl us into the mass grave already dug right under the building.

On the night of July 10, 1971, I became ageless. I have grown neither older nor younger. I have lost my age. You can no longer read it in my face. In fact, I am no longer here to give my age a face. I came to a standstill over in nothingness, where time is abolished, tossed back to the wind, handed over to that vast beach of white sheet rippling in a light breeze, given up to the sky drained of its stars, its images, the childhood dreams that found refuge there, emptied of everything, even God. I crossed over there to learn forgetfulness, but I never succeeded in being completely within nothingness, not even in thought.

Misfortune arrived like a gust of wind, plain as could be, one morning when the sky was blue, so blue that my dazzled eyes could not see for a few seconds, and I hung my head as though it were about to fall off. I knew that very day would be the day of blue stained with blood. I knew it so intimately that I performed my ablutions and prayed in a corner of the barrack room, where a stifling silence reigned. I even said an extra prayer of farewell to life, to springtime, family, friends, dreams, the living. On the hillside across the way, a donkey looked at me with the sad and desolate air of those animals that would like to sympathize with humans in their sorrow. I thought, "At least he has no blood to shed, and no idea that the sky is blue."

Who still remembers the white walls of the palace of Skhirate?* Who remembers the blood on the tablecloths, the blood on the bright green lawn? There was a brutal confusion of colors. The blue was no longer in the sky, the red was no longer on the bodies, the sun was lapping up the blood with extraordinary speed, and we, we had tears in our eyes. Tears that flowed all by themselves and soaked our hands that could not hold a weapon anymore. We were elsewhere, perhaps in the beyond, where eyes roll all the way back into the head. Our eyes were white. We no longer saw sky or sea. A cool wind caressed our skin. The sound of gunfire went on and on into infinity. It was to haunt us for a long time. It would be the only thing we heard. Our ears were busy. I cannot remember anymore whether we surrendered to the royal guard, the one that hunted down rebels, or whether we were arrested and disarmed by officers who had switched sides when the tide turned. We had nothing to say. We were only soldiers, pawns, junior officers too unimportant to take initiatives. We were bodies that were cold in the heat of that summer. Hands tied behind our backs, we were pitched into trucks heaped with the dead and wounded. My head was jammed between two dead soldiers. Their blood was trickling into my eyes. It was hot. Shit and urine were oozing from both bodies. Did I still have the right to be nauseated? I vomited bile. What does a man think of when the blood of other men runs down his face? A flower, a donkey on a hill, a child playing at musketeers with a stick for a sword . . . Perhaps he no longer thinks at all. He tries not to be there, tries to leave his body, to believe he is asleep and trapped in a terrible dream.

No, I knew it was not a dream. My mind was clear. I was shaking all over. I did not hold my nose. I breathed deeply of vomit and death. I wanted to die of suffocation. I tried to stick my head into a plastic bag lying near the bodies. I managed only to anger a soldier who knocked me out with a kick to the back of my head. Losing consciousness, I no longer smelled the stench of the corpses. I couldn't smell anything anymore. I was free. A rifle butt slamming into my shins brought me back to life.

Where were we? It was cold. Perhaps in the morgue of the military hospital in Rabat. The living had not yet been sorted from the dead. Some of the wounded were moaning, others were banging their heads against the wall, cursing fate, religion, the army, and the sun. They were saying the coup d'état had failed because of the sun: it had been too bright, too intense. Others shouted, "But—what coup d'état? Our motto is in our blood: Allah, the Fatherland, the King!" They repeated this slogan like a litany that would atone for their treason.

I kept quiet. I thought nothing. I tried to melt away into the void and no longer hear or feel a thing.

There were twenty-three of us in Cell Block B, each in a separate cell. Besides the hole in the ground that served as a toilet, there was another opening, over the iron door, to let in air. We had no names anymore, no past, no future. Stripped of everything, we had kept only our skins and our heads. Well, not all of us had. Number 12 was the first to lose his reason. He quickly became apathetic. He was way ahead of the rest of us. He entered the house of pain and sorrow by leaving his mind—or what remained of it—at the prison gates. Some claimed they had seen him go through the motions of unscrewing his head and bending down to bury it under two big stones. Admission free, in his case. Nothing got through to him. He talked to himself, nonstop. Even asleep, he kept jabbering incomprehensible words.

Defying explicit orders, we insisted on calling one another only by our given and family names. Number 12's name was Hamid. He was thin and quite tall, with a pasty complexion. His father was an adjutant who had lost an arm in Indochina; the army had undertaken to educate his children, who all became soldiers. Hamid wanted to be an airline pilot and dreamed of leaving the army.

During the day it was impossible to make him be quiet. His delirium reassured us a little: we were still capable of reacting, of wanting to hear words that made sense, that would make us think, smile, or even hope. We knew that Hamid had gone away. He had left us. He neither saw nor heard us anymore. He stared at the ceiling while he talked. In a sense, Hamid was our probable future, even though we had been told over and over that we no longer had a future. Perhaps the doctors had driven him crazy with drugs as an example of what could happen to us. That was not impossible, because during the months spent underground enduring all kinds of torture, some of us lost our lives, and others, like Hamid, our minds.

His voice echoed through the darkness. Now and then we would recognize a word or even a sentence: panther; pot and pothered; possible; poplin; pushcart; pickness; pery pick; pie of punger and pirst . . . It was a letter *P* day.

The guards let him talk, counting on our exasperation to make his presence even more distressing. To foil their game, Gharbi, Number 10, began to recite the Koran, which he knew by heart. He had studied in Koranic school, as had most of us, except that he had intended to become the barracks mufti. He had even entered a recitation contest and won third prize. He was a good Muslim, never missed his prayers, and always said a few verses before going to sleep. At officers' training school, they called him the Ustad, the Master.

When the Ustad began to recite the Koran, Hamid's voice grew softer, softer, until it died away. It was as if the verses of the holy book soothed him, or at least suspended his delirium. The moment the Ustad finished saying the set phrase, "Thus the word of God the All-Powerful is Truth," Hamid began to babble with the same intensity, the same maddening rhythm, the same confusion. No one dared interrupt him. He needed to spout all those words in French and Arabic. It was his way of leaving us, of isolating himself and summoning death, which came for him when he went into a trance and bashed his head against the wall several times. He gave a long cry; then his voice and breath were forever stilled. The Ustad spoke the first sura of the Koran. Sang it, rather. It was beautiful. The silence that fell afterward was magnificent.

The Ustad was chosen to negotiate the conditions of Hamid's funeral with the guards. It was a lengthy and complicated process. The guards had to consult the camp commandant, who had to await instructions from the capital. They wanted to toss the body into a hole without any ceremony, prayers, or reading of the Koran. Our first act of resistance was to demand a decent burial for one of our own. There were twenty-two of us alive, around this body whose voice still sounded in our ears. We invoked the Muslim tradition that frowns on delayed burial, since the sun should set only once on the deceased. Things had to move quickly, especially since the stifling heat—it was September—would soon attack the corpse.

The funeral took place the next morning. Despite the circumstances, we were happy. We were seeing sunlight once more after forty-seven days in darkness. We stood there blinking, and some of us wept. The Ustad performed the ceremony. He asked for water to prepare the body and a sheet to serve as a shroud. Moved, apparently, one of the guards fetched a few canteens of water and a brand-new white sheet.

This was the chance for each of us to try to figure out where we were. I looked for clues. Our building was surrounded by ramparts at least thirteen feet high. One thing was certain: we weren't near the sea. There were gray mountains all around the camp. No trees. A barracks in the distance. Nothing; emptiness. Our prison was half underground. The guards had to be living in two little huts a few hundred yards from where we were burying Hamid.

For one short hour, I kept my eyes and even my mouth wide open, intending to swallow as much light as possible. To breathe in brightness, stockpile it inside, keep it as a refuge, and remember it whenever darkness weighed too heavily on my eyelids. I stripped to the waist so that my skin could absorb and hoard this precious commodity. A guard ordered me to put my shirt back on.

That evening I was ashamed to have been happy thanks to a companion's funeral. Was I pitiless, was I so monstrous that I would take advantage of a death among us? The truth was right there, bitter and brutal. If my neighbor's passing allowed me to see the sun, if only for a few moments, should I wish for his death? And yet, I was not alone in thinking this: Driss, Number 9, had the courage to speak of it. A funeral became for us the opportunity to get out and see daylight. It was our reward, our secret hope, the one you did not dare mention, but thought about.

And death turned into a superb ray of sunshine. We had been dumped there to die, of course. The guards' mission was to keep us on the verge of death for as long as possible. Our bodies were to endure a gradual decomposition. Suffering had to be stretched out over time, allowed to spread slowly, sparing no organ, no patch of skin, rising from the toes to the hair, circulating among the folds, between the wrinkles, insinuating itself like a needle seeking a vein in which to inject its venom.

Let death come! Let the survivors use it to see the light of day! Death's work was well under way. Hamid was the first to offer us a blast of light. It was his parting gift. Gone without suffering, or almost.

After a year in this hole, the question haunting each of us was, "Whose turn is it now?" I had my theories. Driss had a disease of the bones and muscles. He was not meant to have been part of our commando unit. He was even supposed to have been dropped off at the military hospital in Rabat. Our commander forgot. Driss's destiny was to come die in that prison, underground. His withered legs were curled up and clamped to his chest. All his muscles were melting away. He could not lift his hands. The guards allowed me to feed him and help him use the toilet hole. He could no longer chew. I chewed bread and gave it to him in small mouthfuls, followed by a sip of water. Sometimes he choked. Unable to cough anymore, he would bend over, put his head between his legs, and roll on the ground to get the water going the right way into his esophagus. He had gotten so thin he looked like a plucked bird. I couldn't see his eyes very clearly. They must have been glazed, empty. He slept crouching, head resting against the wall, hands wedged under his feet. It took him some time to settle into that position, which allowed him to sleep without too much pain in his joints. He was gradually losing the power of speech. You had to guess at what he was mumbling. I knew that he longed for death. But I could not help him die. In a pinch, if I'd had a little blue pill to set him free, maybe I would have given it to him. Toward the end he refused all nourishment. I felt death making itself at home in his eyes. He tried to tell me something, a number, perhaps. I thought it was the number 40. Death, it seems, takes forty days to occupy the entire body. In his case, it carried him off fairly quickly.

I had a lot of trouble washing the corpse. The folded knees had worn a hole in his rib cage, and the ribs had worked their way into the joints. Impossible to unbend the arms or legs. His body was a ball, all bony. It probably weighed less than ninety pounds. He had become a curious little object so deformed by disease that there was nothing human about him anymore. Before I had even finished preparing the body, I was shoved aside by two guards who returned me to my cell and trundled the corpse away in a wheelbarrow. I was dumbfounded. They had vanished without giving me time to say a single word.

4

It is during grueling hardship that the shabbiest, most ordinary thing becomes exceptional, what you desire most in all the world.

I realized immediately that we had no choice. We had to let go of the simple routines of daily life, forget them, tell ourselves, "My life is over," or, "They've taken away our lives." For us there could be no regrets, no bemoaning our fate, no hope. Life remained outside the double wall surrounding the camp. It is a complete apprenticeship to shed the habits of life, to learn, for example, that days and nights blend together and resemble one another in their hateful dullness. To give up being as you were before. To give up getting out of bed in the morning anticipating the day to come and the surprises it holds for you. No more heading for the bathroom, seeing yourself in the mirror, pulling a face to make fun of Time that leaves a few marks, when you're not looking, on your skin. Spreading the lather on your cheeks and shaving while your thoughts wander idly. Humming, perhaps, or whistling under your breath. Then stepping into the shower and staying there a good fifteen minutes for the modest pleasure of rubbing yourself with lavender-scented soap and feeling hot water pummeling your shoulders. Drying off and slipping into clean undershorts, a nicely ironed shirt, then choosing your suit, tie, shoes. Reading the newspaper while drinking coffee . . . You must let go of these little events in life and never look back. A variation on this scenario: reviewing all the things that won't ever happen to you again. Oh, how do you get used to never brushing your teeth, never tasting that pleasant fluoride flavor in the back of your mouth, having to accept the bad breath, the smells of a neglected body . . . I used almost all of the five quarts of water they gave us to clean myself. Washing in spite of the appalling conditions was an absolute imperative for me. I think that without water I would have come apart. I performed my ablutions to pray and to feel clean, never wiping myself off with the blanket, simply waiting for the water drops to dry.

This apprenticeship was long but very useful. I thought of myself as someone who had been hurled back into the Stone Age and had to reinvent everything with almost nothing.

At first, to amuse myself, I would imagine that providence would perform a miracle, somewhat like those happy endings in American films. I thought of plausible hypotheses: an earthquake; lightning striking all the guards in one fell blow when they gathered under a tree to smoke; the Kmandar, who ran the camp, having a recurring dream in which a heavenly voice would order him to disobey his superiors and set us free, or divine punishment would fall upon his miserable life ... But providence didn't give a damn about our fate. It mocked us with vulgar laughter and angry taunts.

As I was daydreaming, two guards opened my cell door, pounced on me, and stuffed me into a bag, which they dragged toward the exit. I writhed and kicked, my cries smothered by their words: "This one's going to be buried alive—that'll teach the rest of you to shape up!"

The other prisoners howled and pounded on their doors. I struggled with all my might at the bottom of that bag, which was made of extremely stout material. I had the presence of mind to begin reciting the Fatiha,* the first sura of the Koran. I summoned up extraordinary strength. I yelled out the verses so loudly that everyone fell silent. At the end of the corridor, the guards let go of the bag. I heard one of them say to his companion that they had screwed up.

"No, we did what we were told."

"But the Kmandar insisted that he dig his own grave!"

"No, that was a figure of speech. We were just supposed to scare them."

"That's not what I think."

"Listen, we don't have orders to kill, unless there's an attempt to escape."

"You idiot, that's what we were supposed to provoke!"

"No, you've got it all wrong."

"We'll settle this in the Kmandar's office . . ."

While they were arguing, I kept reciting the Koran. They opened the bag and took me back to my cell.

Alone again, I began to laugh hysterically. I could not control myself and calm down. I laughed—laughed and stamped my feet. I knew that this was a provocation, a threat.

My right shoulder ached. In my struggle I must have slammed into a stone. They had complete power over us. What was to keep them from returning and going after someone else, putting him through a mock execution, tossing him into a pit or making him undergo the torment of immobilization? This was a common punishment in the army: bound hand and foot, the victim is buried up to the neck and left exposed to the summer sun or the winter rains.

Perhaps our jailers had in their notebooks a list of mistreatments to inflict on us whenever they pleased. Oddly enough, a few days later, the two guards knocked on my door and asked me not to hold what had happened against them.

"You know, we made a mistake. Actually, when someone is sick or dead, we've been ordered to get rid of him. So, a piece of advice: don't get sick. If you die, it'll be between you and God. In any case, sick or not, nobody gets out of here alive. Better for you if you stay healthy."

I did not reply. They were talking to me, but were really speaking to everyone. We were still in shock from being moved to this new prison. Then I corrected myself, thinking, "Here, I'm not in prison. Here, no one is an inmate serving a sentence. I am—we are—in a dungeon from which no one ever leaves." I remembered the story of Papillon, that French convict who managed to escape from the toughest prison in the world. But I'm not Papillon. I couldn't care less about that guy and his story. Here, we are, I am, I will be—in rebellion. We are at war with an invisible enemy that is everywhere in the darkness. Did I say "enemy"? Correction: here, I have no enemy. I must convince myself of this: no emotion, no hatred, no adversary. I am alone. And I alone can be my enemy. Enough. I file all this away and just stop thinking about it.

5

To remember was to die. It took me some time to realize that the enemy was memory. Anyone who summoned up his past would promptly die. It was as if he had swallowed cyanide. How were we to know that, in that place, homesickness was fatal? We were in our graves, banished forever from our lives and all remembrance. Perhaps the walls weren't thick enough: in spite of the ramparts all around, nothing could keep memory from seeping in. It was so tempting to give in to a daydream of the past, a parade of images that were often rose-colored, some-times hazy, sometimes crystal clear. Raising the specter of a re-turn to life, they would arrive all out of order, fragrant with festivity, or, even worse, with the scents of simple happiness. Ah! The smell of toast and coffee in the morning. Ah! The soft-ness of warm sheets and a woman's hair as she gets dressed again . . . Ah! The shouts of children on a playground, the bal-let of sparrows in a limpid sky, as the afternoon draws to an end! Oh, how lovely and terrible are the simple things in life when they are gone, set forever out of reach! The reveries I gave in to at first were false. I would glamorize the plain facts on pur-pose. Surrounded by darkness, I changed black to living color. It was a game, an insolent one, I thought. All the same, our martyrdom could be relieved by a bit of provocation. I still needed such make-believe to hide the weakness that made me vulnerable. But I was not fooled. The road was long, hard, and treacherous.

You had to agree to lose everything and expect nothing, the better to protect yourself against that eternal night, which was not exactly night but had the same effect, appearance, color, and scent.

It was there to remind us of our frailty.

Unfailing, absolute resistance. All doors shut. Steeling yourself. Forgetting. Emptying the mind of the past. A clean sweep. Nothing left lying around in your head. Never looking back. Learning not to remember anymore. How do you stop this machine? How do you pick and choose in the attic of childhood without becoming a complete amnesiac, without going insane? The thing to do was bolt the doors against everything before July 10, 1971. Not only could they never be opened again, but it was vital to forget what they concealed.

Now I had to feel unaffected by life before that fatal day. Even if words or images broke into my night and prowled around me, I would beat them off, send them packing, because I would be unable to recognize them anymore. I'd tell them: "You've got the wrong person. I have nothing to do with these phantoms. I'm no longer of this world. I have ceased to exist. Yes, it's me speaking. That's precisely it: I'm no longer of this world—of yours, at least, yet I've kept the power of speech and the will to resist, even to forget. The one thing I must not forget is my name. I need it. I'll keep it as a testament, a secret in the gloomy grave where I bear the fateful number: 7." I was seventh in line when we were arrested. It didn't mean much.

My dreams flourished. They visited me often. They would spend part of the night with me, disappear, and leave scraps of daily life in the bottom of my memory. I did not dream of liberation, or of the years before imprisonment. I dreamed of an ideal time, a time suspended among the branches of a celestial tree. If it is the child within us who awakens when we are afraid, here it was the wise man and the lunatic in me who revealed themselves as ardent opponents, each striving to take me the farthest from myself. Smiling placidly, I watched this tug-of-war between two extremes.

Whenever memories threatened to invade me, I would marshal all my strength to bar their way, snuff them out. I'd had to perfect a skillful method to get rid of them. First one must prepare the body to reach the mind: breathe slowly and deliberately from the abdomen; focus oneself by concentrating on this breathing. I allow the images to flood in. I isolate them by chasing away everything moving around them. I blink until they become blurry. Then I stare at one of them for a long time until I freeze it in place. I no longer see anything but this image. I take deep breaths, telling myself that what I see is only a picture that must disappear. In my mind I substitute someone else for me. I must convince myself that I have nothing to do with this image. I tell myself again and again: this memory is not mine. It's a mistake. I have no past, and therefore no memory. I was born and died on July 10, 1971. Before that date I was someone else. What I am now has nothing to do with that other person. Out of respect for his privacy, I do not meddle in his life. I must stay in the background, away from that man who lived before or is living now. I repeat this several times in my head until I see a stranger slowly take my place in the image I have immobilized. This stranger has replaced me beside that young woman who was my fiancée. I know that she is my former fiancée. When did we break up? The moment someone else slipped into this memory and settled in contentedly at her side. I had no way of contacting her. I was completely isolated. I could only communicate in thought with the world above the grave. How could I tell my fiancée not to wait for me anymore, to make her own life and have a child, because I no longer existed? Drastic measures were called for: I have no fiancée anymore. I never had a fiancée. That woman in my memory is an intruder. She broke into my memory, or wound up there through some error. I do not know her. She has nothing whatsoever to do with my life. She and that unknown man who entered the image are strangers to me. It's a photo I must have taken one day while walking in a public park. What park? No. Not even that. Why would I recollect someone I didn't know?

I would go over these obvious facts until I wore out the image, until it faded into oblivion. Similarly, when other images tried to resurface, I would wipe them out by pretending to burn them. I would think, "They don't concern me, they've come to the wrong pigeonhole and the wrong person. It's simple: I don't recognize them and I don't need to." If they persisted, to the point of becoming obsessive, I would beat my head against the wall until I saw stars. By hurting myself, I would forget. The blow on the forehead had the advantage of shattering those images that hounded me and tried to lure me beyond the wall, outside our secret cemetery.

Because of all that pounding, my head became swollen, but also light, since it had been emptied of so many, many memories.

My cell was a tomb. A pit made to slowly swallow up a body. They had thought of everything. I now understood why they had parked us for the first few years in a normal prison, in Kenitra. Normal—in other words a prison you can get out of one day, after serving your sentence. Cells from which you can see the sky, thanks to a window high on the wall. A prison with a courtyard for exercise, where the inmates meet, talk, even make plans. The prison in Kenitra is known for the harshness of its conditions, the toughness of its guards. That's where they lock up the political prisoners. Once I had experienced Tazmamart, Kenitra seemed like an almost human prison in spite of its reputation. There was sunlight there, and a glimmer of hope.

Ten years. That was the sentence we had received. We weren't the ringleaders, just junior officers following orders. But while the pit was being turned into a dying-hole, while the engineers and doctors were studying all the possibilities for prolonging suffering and postponing death until the very last instant, we were in Kenitra, a horrible prison, but a normal one. When they transported us, at night, blindfolded, we had all expected to get a bullet in the back of the head. No. No such luck. Certain death, of course, but not right away. We had to endure—minute by minute—all the physical pains and mental cruelties they inflicted on us. Oh! Sudden death, what a deliverance! A heart attack! A burst aneurysm! A massive hemorrhage! A deep coma! I had wound up hoping for an immediate end. I thought of God again, and of what the Koran says about suicide: everything is in God's hands. Do not hate an evil that might be a blessing. Whoever takes his own life will go to hell and die endlessly the way he killed himself. The hanged man will hang himself forever. Whoever chooses death by fire will live eternally in flames. Whoever jumps into the sea will drown over and over . . .

It was a hot August night in 1973. I was having trouble falling asleep. I could hear my heart beating. It bothered me. I felt a vague sense of dread. I said a few prayers and stretched out on my left side so as not to hear my heartbeats anymore. At around three o'clock, my cell door opened. Three men rushed in: one handcuffed me, another blindfolded me with a black cloth, and the third frisked me, taking my watch and the little money I had. He shoved me into the corridor, where I heard the cries of the other men undergoing the same treatment. They assembled us in the courtyard. The truck engines were running. They called the roll. You had to step forward at your name and serial number. A soldier pushed me over to the short ladder at the back of a truck. Some men protested. The only reply was silence. In a few minutes, we were all inside the covered trucks, en route to an unknown destination. To die. Perhaps it was time to end it all. Going off handcuffed, blindfolded. The image of summary execution. We were all thinking the same thing. A man next to me prayed and even recited his profession of faith, the last words before death: "I testify that there is no God but Allah and that Mohammed is His prophet." He repeated it faster and faster until you couldn't make out a thing—the words were not spoken anymore but mumbled. We were jolted around like crates of vegetables. Obviously, the truck was not traveling on paved road anymore. Soldiers don't like their movements to be noticed or their intentions to be guessed. The ride lasted so many hours that I gave up trying to keep track of the time. I had the impression at one point that the vehicles were going around in a huge circle. In the darkness, the images were white, following one another in a rapid-fire rhythm. Everything was flashing on my screen again: the unbearable glare of Skhirate, the blood drying in the sun, the grayness of the courtroom, our arrival at the prison of Kenitra, and most of all, the face of my mother, whom I had not seen for more than two years but who sometimes appeared to me in a dream.

Of course, like the others, I thought that this voyage into the unknown was our last journey. Curiously enough, I was not frightened. I did not even try to find out where we were. Could the army get rid of fifty-eight people, make them vanish into a mass grave? Who would stand up to defend us and demand justice? We were a special case. Anything was possible. It was better to stop speculating. The trucks kept driving around in circles. Judging from the engine noise, we were climbing a hill—maybe we were on a mountain. It was hot. The air was unbreathable. We were choking. The canvas was too thick and let in dust but very little air. I was thirsty. We all were. When we kept calling out for water, the NCO sitting next to the driver screamed, "Shut your fucking mouths or I'll tape them closed!" We reached our destination during the night. The air was cool, with that freshness that follows the oppressive heat of the day. We heard voices but could not understand what they were saying. Other soldiers must have been coming on duty. We were divided into two groups. I could tell there were a couple of noncoms in Cell Block A. I was assigned to Cell Block B. We were still wearing the blindfolds and handcuffs, which were not removed by guards until the following day.

Alas, when they took off my blindfold, everywhere I looked was black. I thought I had gone blind. We were in a dungeon designed to be in eternal darkness.

6

Faith is not fear, I told myself. Suicide is not a solution. An ordeal is a challenge. Resistance is a duty, not an obligation. Keeping one's dignity is an absolute necessity. That's it: dignity is what I—what we—have left. Each of us does what he can to preserve his dignity. That is my mission. To remain on my feet, be a man, never a wretch, a dishrag, a mistake. I would never condemn those who cannot bear what is inflicted on them, who end by breaking under torture and letting themselves die. I have learned never to judge people. What right would I have to do that? I am only a man, like all others, with the will not to give in. That's all. A will that is firm, ruthless, and uncompromising. Where does it come from? From a long way back. From childhood. From my mother, whom I always saw struggling to raise my brothers and sisters and me. Never giving up. Never flagging for an instant. My mother no longer counted on our father, a bon vivant, a monster of egotism, a dandy who had forgotten he had a family and gave all his money to tailors who sewed him a new silk djellaba* every week. He had his shirts sent from England, his babouches* from Fez, his perfume from Paris or Saudi Arabia, and he strutted about in the palaces of the El Glaoui family. Meanwhile, my mother toiled away, working every day of the week so that we should want for nothing. We had the bare essentials. Only her youngest, whom she called her lambkin, was entitled to be spoiled. My mother's strictness melted away before her little prince, an astonishing child of glowing intelligence and countless caprices. Nothing was denied him, not even a moped for his fifteenth birthday. And then there was that confession at the supper table between two peals of laughter: "Mama, I like men better than women—I'm in love with Roger, my literature teacher!" Ah! The little prince! We all doted on him, perhaps because our mother adored him, and we did not want to aggravate her or contest her way of taking joy in this child. She was amazed at his beauty and his extraordinary gaiety. The day she sent our father packing, she gathered us all together and warned us: "No lazy bones in my house, and no class dunces. From now on, I'm your mother and your father!"

When he married my mother, my father was a jeweler in the medina* of Marrakech. He had inherited this shop from his maternal uncle, who was childless and considered him his son. My father spent his time reading and learning by heart the works of the great Arab poets, pausing only to charm the beautiful women who stopped to admire the jewelry in his display window. He was known for his penchant for seduction and his poor business sense. In any case, he planned to teach literature at the University of El Qaraouiyne in Fez. After his father was summoned to the court of Pasha El Glaoui, however, he closed the shop and followed him to the palace, where he taught Arabic to the children and grandchildren of the pasha.

This happened early in the 1950s. The pasha was a friend of the French, with whom he collaborated. Like his own father, who claimed he never meddled in politics, my father must have pretended not to be aware of what was said in nationalist circles.

This father whom I hardly knew was in fact a poet and the friend of poets, a lover of elegance and ostentation who craved the friendship of the powerful and the pleasure of making them laugh. He had no sense of family and felt no responsibility for his many children. Toward the end of the 1960s, thanks to his phenomenal memory, his unfailingly quick wit, and his traditional education (he could recite thousands of verses by Ben Brahim* without a single mistake), he became the king's court jester, and then his friend. I was already in the army when one of my brothers told me the news. "The king no longer lets our father out of his sight. They've become close friends! Now we never see him anymore. He's always at the palace. Even when the king is traveling, he takes him along."

So the dandy of Marrakech, the Don Juanesque seducer, the living memory of popular poetry, the man who had made my mother suffer so much, who thought only of his pleasure, the jeweler of the medina, homesick for the court of Pasha El Glaoui, that man who was capable of not recognizing one of his own offspring if he met the child in the street, the man called "the scholar," "the master," was really just the king's clown. As far as my mother was concerned, that man no longer existed. She had decided to live as if he were dead. She never spoke of him. And we were forbidden to mention this absent father, a man who cared more about matching the color of his babouches to his djellaba than about the chaotic school attendance of his youngest child.

Serving the king. Being at his feet. At his beck and call. Never going to bed before he did. Telling him stories, cheering him up when he was feeling low. Finding *les mots justes,* the words suiting the occasion. Giving up having your own life. Being constantly at the mercy of his moods. And most important, having to be funny at all times.

Despite the burlesque aspect of his office, he played an important role close to the king. Certain people in the royal entourage would confide their grievances to my father so that he might pass them along whenever his master was disposed to listen to them. People consulted my father on the state of the king's temper. My father would wear a big smile to broadcast the message, "His Majesty is in a good humor today!"

He was a court jester, and he must have been quite proud of this. It was the crowning glory of a long career and the realization of another dream: to be for the king what his father had been for Pasha El Glaoui. I have been describing my father because on July 10, 1971, he did remember that I was his son. He was among the guests at that birthday party at the palace of Skhirate, where dignitaries, diplomats, and government officials would be mowed down, machine-gunned by an entire platoon of young cadets. I myself did not fire my weapon. I was in shock. We had all gone crazy: sickened, disgusted, and already crushed, perhaps dead, although we did not yet know it. That is what I had realized. I was a dead man at the very moment I entered the summer palace. I was dead and I didn't care. Everything was spinning around me: the people, the tables, the guns, the blood in the water of the swimming pool, the stars in the morning sky, and above all the sun, pursuing us relentlessly.

A few days later, when my father learned that I had been among the attackers, he scratched his cheeks with his fingernails to display his shame and threw himself at the king's feet to embrace them, weeping. When the king reached out to help him rise, my father disowned me with these words.

"God gave me a son, twenty-seven years ago. I ask God to take him back. May He summon him and cast him into hell. In the name of Allah the All-Powerful, in my soul and conscience, in all serenity, I disown this unworthy son, I consign him to public condemnation, to eternal obliteration, I strip my name from him, I throw him into the gutter so that rats and mad dogs can rip out his heart, his eyes, his liver, and tear him into pieces to be thrown into the sea of utter oblivion. God is my witness, and you, Majesty, are my witness, as I say and say again: this son is no longer mine. He does not exist anymore. He has never existed. May Your Majesty throw me as well into the vast ocean of oblivion, because I have been soiled by this outrage and no longer deserve to be your servant, your slave. Send me away, speak but one word and you will never again see this face that dares not lift itself to your countenance, this face that has lost all color, all identity, and become the face of shame itself. In my eyes this worthless son is dead. May he be brought back to life to suffer, to pay until his last hour for the unspeakable offense he tried to commit against royalty, God, and His humble servant. I reject him, I reject him, I reject him! I curse him, I curse him, I curse him! How, O my God, can I beg for your pardon? How, O Majesty, can I solicit your aid? Not to save this man, who betrayed God, who stabbed the fatherland and had the absolute audacity, the unimaginable folly, to make an attempt on your life, a life as noble, as good, as lofty as the sky! He attacked you, the Commander of the Faithful, you, a direct descendant of our Prophet! How, Majesty, can I beg for your help to continue to live, to no longer keep my eyes cast down, eyes bruised by the offense, the insult, the betrayal of my own offspring? O my master, O our Lordship, Your Majesty, I surrender to you, a bound slave. Let His Majesty do with his servant as he will. I am his. I have no more family. I have no more children. I am at His Majesty's feet!"

The king murmured an order and disappeared, leaving my father distraught, crouching with his hands held out before him as a sign of the utmost submission.

I do not think the king was in a state to hear anything else. Later I was told that he asked my father to keep him company at night from then on and to recite poems by Ben Brahim until he fell asleep, which was usually only in the early hours of the morning, between four and five o'clock. After making sure that his master was drifting gently into slumber, my father would rise and silently back out of the bedchamber, on tiptoe.

I did not learn all that until a few months after my release from prison.

I now ask myself the question that haunted me for eighteen years, although I never dared put it in words, for fear of going insane or sinking into fatal depression, which did afflict some of us and cause them to waste away. The question no longer frightens me. I even find it pointless, but not without interest: when I rushed into the summer palace with the rest of the cadets, whom was I trying to kill—the king or my father?

7

Back to the pit. Total darkness. Even the opening in the ceiling is shielded; air can enter, but we cannot see daylight.

Karim was Number 15. He was a short, fat man, from El Hajeb. Many soldiers, noncoms, and even officers have come from that area. In his family they were army from father to son. He had no choice. All his brothers were simple soldiers. He wanted to become an officer. The school in Ahermemou was what he dreamed of when he did his training at the camp in El Hajeb.

He was someone who spoke little, smiled even less, but was obsessed by a single thing: time. He could tell what time it was to within a minute, day or night. So he was perfectly cut out to be our calendar, our clock, and our link with the life left behind us, or above our heads. He was afraid that if he started a discussion with one of us he would lose track of the time. Some amused themselves by testing him: "What time is it?" And especially, "What day of what month is it?"

As if a button had been pushed, the talking clock would speak up: "It's 1975, May 14, at exactly 9:36 in the morning."

I suggested to my companions that they stop disturbing him for no reason. He would announce the hour three times a day, just so that we could orient ourselves mentally in the black hole and have the illusion of mastery over time.

This gave Karim a permanent full-time job. To us he was Time, without the anguish that would be created by the blind pursuit of a phantom chopped up into minutes, hours, days . . . He was calm. Serene. Being the guardian of time's passage let him feel as though he did not belong to our group. He was an unassuming man, without arrogance. He had found his place in the shadows. His discretion and punctuality impressed us. He never said a word about our situation. He had become the clock and the calendar, and nothing in the world would have induced him to abandon this post. It was his way of surviving: to withdraw, supervising the tempo of a time forbidden to us. Strangely enough, becoming time's slave had set him free. He was out of reach, completely enclosed by his bubble, unencumbered by anything that might distract him and disrupt his timekeeping. He was forced to be methodical. It was his mission, his life buoy.

As for me, I quickly discovered that the instinct of self-preservation would not help me survive. That instinct we share with animals was now out of order as well. How could one stay alive in that hole? Why bother dragging this body, broken and disfigured, into the light? We had been placed in conditions designed to prevent our instinct from envisaging the future. I realized that time had meaning only in the movement of beings and things, whereas we were reduced to the immobility and eternity of the material world. We were in a motionless present. The unfortunate soul who looked back or peered into the future rushed headlong into death. The present left only enough space for its own unfolding. You had to keep to the immutable instant, and not think about it. A realization that doubtless saved my life.

I would never have thought that a simple broom could prove so useful. The guards refused to enter our hole to sweep up the garbage. Each of us took his turn at housekeeping. The guards would open the door of one lockup and then leave. They said they did not want to be contaminated by our germs. We were dirty, unshaven, and our prison was kept in a state of filthiness conducive to every disease. While he was sweeping one day, Lhoucine, Number 20, cried out in what sounded almost like joy. He came over to my cell to speak to me.

"Hey, the broomstick has an iron tip!"

"So what? That's why you're shouting?"

"But it's metal! If I can pull it off, we could make a knife from it, then a razor . . ."

That is how Lhoucine and I came to spend about ten days

working on the metal tip, passing it back and forth. We flattened and then sharpened it on a hard stone until it had a thin, keen edge. Next we decided to cut our hair, each in turn, and some removed their beards as well. Meanwhile, Abdullah, Number 19, had swiped the tip of another broom. I knew the expression "to get a dry shave," used when someone has been badly cheated. In my case, it was not a figure of speech. I shaved with no soap and very little water. I had a heavy beard, which I cut tuft by tuft. I had no mirror, obviously, and even if I'd had one, there was no light. I shaved like a blind man. I had become a blind man. And how could you convince me otherwise? I saw without seeing. I imagined more than I saw.

The blade traveled from hand to hand. Operation Haircut lasted a good month. Lhoucine, who was particularly clever with his hands, made five needles out of the other blade. He spent hours honing it until it was quite thin, so thin that he could slice pieces off with the first razor blade and even dig out tiny holes for the thread.

We were cold and had no change of clothes. We had been lightly clad when we were arrested that day in July, and we were still wearing our summer uniforms.

We had the presence of mind to keep the shirts and trousers of those who died. Now, with a needle, we could mend tears and even sew two or three vests for our weakest companions.

The cold was a deadly enemy. It attacked us with a harshness that gave us the shakes or the runs. That last is hard to explain, as cold does not normally cause diarrhea—fear does. When the bitter cold arrived, our hands would stiffen, and our joints became inflexible as well. We could not even rub our hands together or pass them over our faces. We were as rigid as corpses. But we had to stand up, and I would get to my feet, with my head and shoulders slumped forward. Sometimes I would stay hunched over and walk back and forth in my cell along the diagonal. The cold interfered with my thinking. It made me hear friendly voices, like a mirage for a man lost in the desert. The freezing cold muddled everything. It was an electric drill piercing holes in the skin. No blood spurted out; it had frozen in the veins. It was vital to keep our eyes open, stay awake. Those so feeble they succumbed to sleep died within a few hours. Blood did not circulate anymore. It was gelid. Ice in the brain and the heart. Keeping alert, moving our feet, hopping, talking, talking to ourselves: that's how we fought the penetrating cold. By not thinking about its bite anymore—denying it, refusing it.

Baba, the Saharawi who joined our group one evening, froze to death. There were two of them, tall and skinny. The other one's name was Jama'a. He never spoke. They had arrived exhausted, probably after being tortured. They could hardly walk. A guard threw them each into a cell.

"You sons of bitches!" he shouted. "I've brought you company—some bigger sons of bitches, since they're even worse traitors than you are. They say the Sahara doesn't belong to Morocco!"

We hadn't heard about this business with the Sahara. We were in solitary confinement, and the few times we did get some news were when the guards felt like talking about their friends at the front. During the Green March,* we were underground. Every now and then, a guard would threaten us.

"You could be useful—walking out in front to sweep the road full of mines buried by rotten bastards, those mercenaries paid by Algeria to swipe our Sahara. At least then, if people got blown sky-high after stepping on mines, it wouldn't be our brave soldiers but you lousy traitors."

It took several days to deal with Baba's death. The guards thought he was sleeping. The man in a cell next to his told them he could not hear him breathing anymore. They poked Baba with their gun barrels, trying to wake him up. He had stopped moving. He was dead, all right. I should note that one of the guards did say, "We belong to God and to Him we must return." We began to recite the Koran out loud. Unable to bear that dismal funeral litany, the guards left. The sky was dark gray. It was raining. The burial was a hurried affair. It felt a little less cold outside than inside.

Baba had arrived wearing a blue tunic. It was long and wide, the traditional dress of the desert people. We had salvaged it— to be more precise, we had grabbed it away from the guards. With that cloth, Lhoucine and I sewed three pairs of trousers, five shirts, and four pairs of underpants. How could one help thinking that Baba's death was a boon to those he left behind? We blessed him and prayed a long time for the salvation of his soul. Baba had come from the deep south of Morocco to die among us. His companion Jama'a had a hard, impassive face. When he realized where he was and that this hole was our common grave, he let out a powerful cry that seemed to go on forever. Then he began singing the songs of his tribe, after which he sank into a deep silence that lasted several days and nights. He did not sleep. His great height was a problem, and he crouched uncomfortably, now and then murmuring something unintelligible.

Finally, listening one time when Karim announced the date and the hour, Jama'a felt at peace, and spoke to us.

"When I cried out, it was because I couldn't tell if it was day or night. It's enough to drive you insane. Now I know what's going on. Forgive me, my brothers, for this cry that must have been painful to your ears. I was enraged. We stupidly let ourselves be caught. A trap. We were betrayed. Baba was the person I loved best in all the world, and now that he's dead, nothing matters to me anymore. I believed in the revolution. We even thought we could inspire the Moroccan people to join us. But we were mistaken, manipulated by Algerians, Cubans . . . Me, I was born in Marrakech. I'm like you. When they came to recruit me, I was enthusiastic. They told me, 'Revolution always rises in the south.' So I went south: I changed my name and joined the Saharawi army."

He was talking to stay awake. And we listened to him. But I was thinking about something else. I was dreaming about getting a piece of his blue tunic. I had given everything away to others and I was cold, my testicles were aching terribly. I tried to warm them with my hands, but my joints were almost frozen, so my hands could not cup my genitals for very long. With a piece of material, at least I could make a sort of bandage to cover them. I waited until he had finished his story, then asked him for some of his tunic. When I heard, in the quiet darkness, the lovely sound of tearing cloth, I jumped for joy, banging my head on the ceiling.

"I'll wad it up into a ball and throw it," he told me.

Just as in a movie thriller, the rolled-up cloth did not land in my cell, but right in front of my door. How could I get it? With what? If the guards saw the cloth, they would confiscate it. Lhoucine reminded me that we still had the broom, which was passed to me from cell to cell. Then the search began. A blind broom in blind hands! I was flat on my stomach, slowly sticking out the broomstick, trying to locate this piece of material. It took a full hour to retrieve it, and then it was my turn to give the Saharawi yell, which sounds like Indians shouting in victory over the American cavalry.

That night, I did not sleep. I wrapped myself up in the cloth, which protected me a little from the chill. The next day, I set to work making what I needed to fight the awful cold.

8

On the outside, when a cup of coffee is crummy, people say, "It's sock juice." In the early days of our imprisonment, I used that expression. I was mistaken. Sock juice has a taste, a smell—bad, of course, but you can drink it and even ask for more. What they served us in the morning was lukewarm water mixed with powder made from some sort of scorched starchy substance. Impossible to determine which one. Maybe chickpeas, maybe red beans. It was not coffee, or tea. The question was unanswerable. The stuff hit your stomach like a vomitory. An enema? She-camel piss mixed with the commandant's urine? We just swallowed it and stopped wondering what it was.

Bread. Yes, we were entitled to bread as white as quicklime. Guaranteed the minimum caloric intake to prevent starvation. I have often conjured up the image of a doctor busily calculating the number of calories we needed, having his report typed up by a secretary with bright red lipstick and a classic chignon hairdo, and delivering it to the officer who had requested it from him. The bread was shaped like an automobile tire. Hard. Dense. Tasteless. With that loaf, skillfully thrown, you could kill someone. The bread was cement. You did not cut it, you broke it. You did not chew it, you gnawed it. Since most of us had bad teeth, eating this bread was an extra torment. Some kept the liquid from the morning so they could dunk their bread ration in it. Others broke the bread into small chunks and poured the daily plate of starch over them.

Starch. O starchy foods, my sadness, my companions, my visitors, my compulsory menu, my survival, my personal abomination, my worn-out burned-up tossed-aside love, my ration of calories, my obsessive madness! Starches that I eat and pass through my stomach with something like pleasure.

Starches morning and evening. It was like a doctor's prescription. Above all, no change. No variety. The body must get used to eating the same starches until death. Stale bread, and starches cooked in water without oil or spices. Once a week, they were cooked in camel fat. It stank. I ate holding my nose. I preferred—if this word still had meaning in that hole—starches cooked in water.

We were all on the same diet: the same starches served to death.

So, for eighteen years, more precisely, for 6,663 days, I was nourished only on starchy food and dry bread. Never any meat. Never any fish. Nourished is not the word. Kept alive. It did not take me long to forget about cigarettes. I didn't even suffer through the miserable deprivation that drove Larbi—Number 4—off his head. He would scream, rip his only shirt, call the guards, offer them anything at all for a cigarette.

"Even if you won't give me a cigarette, come smoke next to me, let me inhale that smoke I miss so much. Take whatever you want . . . Yes, I know, I haven't got anything . . . Maybe my ass . . . You can have it, it's only bones, but a puff, just one puff, then you waste me, blow my ass away, I'll take off like a rocket for chain smokers' hell. Come over here, forget we're enemies, and remember, we're from the same village, if you slip me a cigarette you could go to my house and they'll give you some money and clothes . . ."

Poor Larbi went on a hunger strike and let himself die. For a month we heard him moaning softly.

"I want to die. Why is death taking so long? Who's holding him up, who's keeping him from coming down here and sliding under my cell door? It's the guard with the mustache, the mean one, he's barring the way. It's so hard to die when you're begging for death! He doesn't care about my fate. But let him through, give him a good welcome! This time, he's coming for me. To set me free. Listen, the rest of you, don't grab him as he goes by. I see him, he's finally answered my call. Farewell, cadets! Farewell, revolutionaries! Farewell, friends! I'm out of here, no doubt about it, I'm off, and over there I'm going to smoke a cigarette that just never ends . . ."

Death stood him up. Did not carry Larbi off until a whole week after the night he thought he had spotted him. Larbi was a good guy, a perpetual worrywart, obliging, and a touch simpleminded. At Ahermemou, he was among those at the bottom of the class. Right before the coup d'état he was supposed to have been transferred back to El Hajeb, where he would have wound up as a noncom. It was only a matter of days. He could not manage to keep up. His file had been forgotten, and the day we set out, he got into the truck with the others, without knowing where he was going or why. When he smoked a cigarette, you would have thought he was chewing it. It was probably his only pleasure.

He had lost so much weight he did not seem human anymore. His eyes were bloodshot and bulged from their sockets. There was foam at the corners of his mouth. In that bony face you could read all the hatred and distress in the world. Gharbi, the Ustad, recited the Koran during his burial. The light was terrifying, which is to say superb, magnificent. It was springtime. I filled my eyes and lungs with that light. So did everyone else. Gharbi stopped for a few minutes, closed his eyes, breathed deeply, then opened his mouth as if he were eating air. The guards let us take advantage of that funeral for a little while longer. We thanked Larbi, saying, "Farewell, goodbye, see you soon! We'll meet again over there, we'll throw ourselves on God's mercy, we belong to Him, and to Him we will return." Of that I had no doubt. I did not belong to the king, or to the commandant of the underground cemetery, or to the guards armed to the teeth. I belonged only to God. He alone would receive my soul and judge me. The cruelty of these soldiers no longer concerned me. I believed more and more in God, Allah the All-Powerful, Allah the Compassionate, the Most High, the Merciful, He who knows the heavens and the earth, He who knows what is in our hearts and where souls go.

That light, on that April day, was a sign of His goodness. It had soothed me, calmed me, and I was ready to go back into my hole.

I volunteered to clean out Larbi's cell. To overcome the stench of shit and sickness, I thought only of the light and the springtime. I did not even have to hold my breath, I was there and elsewhere at the same time. I hummed as though I were happy. I had decided to renounce sadness and hatred, just as I had renounced memory.

I scrubbed the floor, where a mash of bread crusts and food debris had fermented. The cell reeked of vomit and mould. The odor had to have a color. I imagined it as greenish, with reddish-brown spots. Perhaps everything was black and I was wasting my time adding color where there was nothing but grayness and decay.

It was a good spiritual exercise for me. Back in my cell, I washed myself and felt a cozy sense of well-being. It was as if comfort meant simply not smelling putrid garbage.

9

Most of those who died did not die of hunger but of hatred.

Feeling hatred diminishes you. It eats at you from within and attacks the immune system. When you have hatred inside you, it always crushes you in the end. I had to go through this ordeal to understand something that simple. I remember an instructor at the school in Ahermemou who was a bad man, spiteful and gloomy. He had yellow eyes. The color of hate. One day, he did not come to class. We learned he was in the hospital for a long stay. I don't recall what had happened to him, but people said he had been bewitched by a mountain woman whose daughter he had raped.

How could we not feel hatred, with everything they made us go through? How could we be greater, more noble than those faceless brutes? How could we get beyond those cravings for vengeance and destruction?

When it struck me that some of our first companions to die were possessed by hatred, I understood that they had been its earliest victims. The one who convinced me of this was Rushdie, Number 23, a gentle, serious man, subtle and intelligent. I used to tell myself he had mistaken his calling. What was he doing in the army? He was from an important family in Fez, bourgeois who detested the army. I believe they thought only the sons of peasants and mountain people should be soldiers. This family's children were destined for universities and careers as higher civil servants or perhaps important businessmen. Rushdie came from this background and did not like to be reminded of it. He had joined the army to rebel against his parents—to forget his origins, tear up his roots, leave his rather aristocratic education behind, and explore different social spheres. There was friendship between us, and a sense of complicity. I think that only Rushdie and I suspected that Commandant A. was planning a coup d'état. When they ordered us into the trucks, we looked at each other. Our eyes were shining. Tears, perhaps, or the feverish anticipation of an unknown adventure. We noticed a long private conversation between the commandant and Atta, his trusty adjutant. A heavy silence lasted through the entire ride. Rushdie smoked one cigarette after another. He kept his head bowed. I think he was crying.

Rushdie was in shock, traumatized. As we invaded the palace, he told me he was going to surrender. He was shaking. He fell, crumpled up around his weapon, and was shot in the shoulder, losing consciousness. When we saw each other again in prison in Kenitra, he told me he did not understand why he was there. He said he hadn't done anything and that it was a horrible mistake, an injustice. I gave up trying to reason with him. All he talked about was killing and revenge. He had caught hatred as though it were an incurable disease. He wanted to slaughter everyone: the guards, the judge, the lawyers, the royal family, all those behind his incarceration. When we were transferred to Tazmamart, he went out of his mind fairly quickly. He no longer knew what he was saying, but remained obsessed by hatred. It undermined him, ate away at him, made him a stranger to himself. No one died during that period, so we could not see one another. I often called to him. No answer. Only cries, the shrieks of a wounded animal. He, too, wanted to hasten death, but death, in league with our jailers, was taking its own sweet time.

One day, I asked a guard to let us see him, only for a moment. It wasn't a question of getting out of the hole, but of borrowing the guard's flashlight and visiting Rushdie. I received a stinging refusal, along with threats and insults. So we went on strike.

No talking. We observed perfect silence in the dungeon. Not one word. Not one movement. We controlled our breathing. A

few minutes of profound quiet, eerie and oppressive, drove the
guards wild. They yelled and pounded on the doors with the
butts of their weapons. We played dead. Silence plus darkness
made a recipe favorable to the appearance of djinns.* It never
failed.

"Let's go!" shouted one of the guards. "Let's get the fuck out
of here! This place is haunted—I swear, I saw a djinn with glowing eyes . . . Let's leave these bastards with the djinns, they're all
the same scum. Come on, quick . . ."

Off they went with a bellyful of fear, while we gloated
shamelessly, cackling like djinns.

We did not see Rushdie again before he died. The guard who
came to confirm his death was petrified. Shining a light on the
dead man's face, he recoiled with a cry of horror and fled, dropping his flashlight, which we maneuvered close to one of the cells
with the handle of our famous broom, only to find it would not fit
under the door. When another guard appeared to restore order, he
said nothing, just assigned Lhoucine and me to prepare the
corpse. He then arranged to have the burial take place at night.
He must have been an NCO. His name was M'Fadel. When we
were all gathered around the body, he said a few words.

"The next time you go on strike, I'll let loose scorpions. And
then we'll see who's the real djinn, you or me! All right, stick
this fucking shit in the hole."

As one man, we responded by reciting the Fatiha. The guards
shoved us violently toward the door to the hole while M'Fadel
pissed on a big stone.

Our talking clock was out of order. Karim must have been
very affected by that nighttime funeral, and especially upset by
the NCO's threats. He had lost track of time. We could hear
him, fretting in his cell, tallying up the days and hours of the
week. I advised him to calm down, assuring him that things
would all fall back into place. He went to sleep, and the next
morning, he awakened us by imitating a crowing rooster.

"It's five o'clock, it's the dawn prayer, O my brothers in faith,
O Muslims, awake, prayer does not wait!"

Then, after a moment, he continued.

"Sleep no more, sleep no more, my brothers, pay attention, it's summertime, today is July 3, 1978, it's 5:36 A.M., it's scorpion time. Be very careful, they're here, I feel them, I hear them. After the bitter cold and dampness, summer has arrived, the summer of scorpions. We must get organized. My machine almost broke down because I sensed an alien presence in my cell. No, it isn't djinns. No, they're killers, vermin that sting and release their poison."

I became a scorpion expert. I understood them without having studied them. I knew how they move, the noise they make, at what temperature they sting, where they love to hide, and how they fool their adversaries.

I knew all that by intuition. We could not see them in the darkness. This was the first summer they had appeared. And not in a natural way. Not by chance. The NCO had brought them into the hole. I was sure of it. Because how could you explain this sudden invasion after five summers without these terrifying creatures? But how could that guy have done such a thing? I really could not imagine a lieutenant colonel or a general meeting with other officers at headquarters to order some flunky to go collect scorpions and dump them in our pit. No, it had to be someone's personal initiative. This NCO—maybe he was a staff sergeant—was taking revenge, not from any love of the monarchy, but from hatred for his superiors who had posted him there to guard the living dead, or should I say the barely surviving condemned to a slow death.

As Karim had said, we had to get organized. We held a meeting after our evening ration of starches. We were all standing in our respective cells. Me, I was squatting, because I was so tall. Number 21, Wakrine, a decent fellow, told us that he had played with scorpions when he was a boy in Tafraout, a particularly hot and arid region. He said the scorpion is vicious but not very smart; it likes to cling to rocks, but if it falls, it stings.

He was right. We had to be quiet, absolutely quiet, to locate the scorpions. As long as we heard them walking, we knew they were overhead, and if they dropped, we had to tell from the noise which side they were on and move away from them. To do that you had to stay awake. My friend Lhoucine was stung when he drifted off to sleep. We called the guards, who came only the following morning, when they brought what they referred to as "coffee." Wakrine begged the guards to let him suck out the venom. Poor Lhoucine was already delirious with a raging fever.

"The fever will last forty-eight hours," Wakrine told us, spitting out the poison. "It always does. Whatever you do, don't fall asleep."

"We're all dying of exhaustion!" someone shouted.

"We'll crack up!" wailed someone else.

"This scorpion business is a plot to kill us off quickly," announced my neighbor on the right.

"But the authorities wouldn't like that," I replied, "because they want to see us die by inches."

"Screw what the authorities think," said Ustad Gharbi calmly. "I'm even certain that everyone has forgotten us—the ones who sentenced us and the ones who threw us into this grave. The problem now is to demand some light from the guards to drive these killers from our cells."

Light, obviously! But the whole system was based on the principle of darkness, on that unfathomable obscurity, the gloom that heightened fear of the invisible, fear of the unknown. Death was on the prowl. It was near. But we were not to know from which direction it would strike, or with what weapon. We were meant to be at the mercy of the unseen. That was the torture, the sophistication of their revenge.

I had thought it over many, many times. All right, we did try to kill him. We searched everywhere among the guests for him.

We lost our gamble. We ourselves were just soldiers, subordinate officers trapped in the frenzy of that hell, carrying out orders. Why didn't they kill us right away? Even in a country like France, the man who shot at General de Gaulle's car was executed. That's normal. Why did they try us in a courtroom and sentence us to ten years in prison only to condemn us to a lingering death? Why were the generals, the ones who planned the coup d'état, stripped of their rank and sent before a firing squad, while we, the junior officers, the cadets' instructors—we had to undergo the endless agony of creeping death? A vicious, perverse death that tormented our nerves and what little we had left: our dignity. What good did it do to drag everything out? We had been swept up in the wake of men who had committed a wrong, a crime. Why keep us alive? Why turn us into the living dead, providing just enough oxygen for us to survive and suffer?

The day will come when I will feel no hatred, when I will finally be free and will reveal everything I have endured. I will write it down or have someone else write it, not for revenge, but for the record, to add a document to our history file. Meanwhile, I try to talk, to talk to myself, to keep from falling asleep and becoming easy prey for the scorpions. I talk, I hop, I bump my head gently against the wall. I think I know where my scorpion is holed up. My sharp hearing has told me that it must be between the third and fourth stones in the crack where the rain comes through during a downpour. I huddle over on the other side. I'm confident, betting on my intuition. If I am stung, Wakrine will suck out the venom. He's used to it. I'm getting drowsy. I hold my breath. Nothing moves. Tough, I can't help it; crouching there, I nod off . . .

I was awakened by a stabbing pain in my back. It was not a scorpion sting. My backache had returned. Rheumatism? Slipped disk? Muscle cramp? How could I tell? Being constantly bent over must deform the spine somehow. What good would it do to find what caused the pain? I had to bear it, live with it, and try to forget it. Each of us had some part of his body or mind that had completely deteriorated. All our illnesses, all our problems had grown worse. No doctor. That was the rule. Doctors had no business there. Everyone knows the doctor's job is to struggle against death, beat it back, even defeat it. There, the goal was precisely the opposite. If disease showed up, it was allowed to gain a foothold, develop, take over the entire body, contaminate healthy organs, do its work and inflict every aspect of suffering on the body. All medical attention was forbidden. Anyway, we had no one to speak or complain to, the way we'd had in the prison in Kenitra.

There was an officer at Tazmamart, a commandant. We never saw him. He must have been a phantom, a shadow, someone who had to be there but did not need to show himself. Perhaps he was a voice barking a series of harsh orders against which there was no appeal. A recorded voice, probably an actor's. When they were in a good mood, the guards would promise to speak to the Kmandar—that is how they pronounced it—but we never received answers to our requests. From which we concluded: the Kmandar did not exist. He was merely a scarecrow, and we pretended he was there, a few dozen yards from the camouflaged entrance to our hole. How could such special prisoners be entrusted to a Kmandar who might find himself one evening sitting at the bar in some dive in Marrakech or Casablanca, fueled by alcohol and remorse, and begin talking, saying the frightening name of this little village, Tazmamart, located between Rachidia and Rich on the map of Morocco?

The Kmandar, the invisible officer, was Terror. The guards spoke of him as if he were a chunk of metal, inflexible, inhuman, all powerful. They said, "The Kmandar, he's made of iron. *Hédid*—hard as steel!"

Later, much later, one day when I found myself face to face

with the Kmandar, I realized that this person had been sculpted from some special material, a kind of bronze or indestructible metal.

He was born to serve, to carry out all assignments, from the most ordinary to the most monstrous of tasks. Without any emotion. Without any doubts. He received orders and implemented them with a metallic firmness. Before being put in charge of us, he had already slit the throats of several wretches, buried others alive, tortured opponents of the regime with the application of a specialist. He had lost an eye in a car accident. It was God's will, he said. That's all.

Of the eight guards, two were particularly bad. There was Fantass, a tall, thin man with gold teeth. He spat constantly and was truly nasty. When he spoke, he used only vulgar, insulting words. We did not answer, leaving him to his foul temper. Later we learned he used to report his colleagues who were not mean enough to us, accusing them of weakness and even sympathy with "the dogs and traitors."

One day, Fantass disappeared. We no longer heard his hoarse voice or the hiss of his spitting. Two months later, when he returned, we hardly recognized him. He opened each cell and asked for forgiveness. I could see his features thanks to the flashlight he held pointed toward his face. He wept, and made a strange confession.

"I'm sorry, I did bad things, horrible things. I spat in your grub and threw sand in it. I hated you because I'd been taught to hate. I hoped you'd die slow, painful deaths. I deserve to go to hell for the evil I did to you. God has punished me! He just snatched away my two grown children, killed instantly in a brand-new car. This is God's justice. I have nothing more to do here below. I'm going to die as well. It's all over for me. Help me to go by forgiving me!"

Fantass died a few months later, after a hunger strike.

Another guard, Hmidouche, was also quite mean. He'd had a fall, and limped. When he saw what had happened to his friend

Fantass, he became scared and started asking us to forgive him as well! The other guards said nothing; they stayed away from us as much as possible. They were afraid of M'Fadel, their boss.

It was pointless to say, "I'm sick, I don't feel well this morning, I'm a bit under the weather . . ." So, why bother thinking or saying it? Illness was our normal, permanent condition. We were to lose a little of our health with each passing day until the end, until extinction. We had two assets: our bodies and our minds. I quickly decided to use all possible means to save my brain. I began to protect my conscience and intellect. The body was exposed; in a way, it belonged to our captors, was in their power. They tortured it without touching it, amputating a limb or two simply by denying us medical care. But my thoughts had to remain out of reach: that was my real survival, my freedom, my refuge, my escape. To stay alive my mind needed training, gymnastics. I had removed and even erased memories that could drag me toward the abyss; in the same way, I decided to exercise my intellect by being lucid, absolutely and ferociously lucid. I had one chance in a hundred of getting out of there. Not much to count on. If a miracle turns up, I thought, I'll be reborn, with a new lease on life at the age of forty or fifty. But I wasn't banking on it. I would get out of the hole and go touch the black stone of the Kaaba* in Mecca. It was that black stone—the stone of the beginning, the one that still shows Abraham's footprints, the one whose memory is linked with the memory of the world—that saved me. I believe this even today. I do not know why my thoughts were fixated on this symbol. I made it my reference point, my window onto the other side of the night. I would open this window and see something radiant.

The fact of centering myself, mastering the rhythm of my breathing, focusing on an idea, an image, a sacred stone thousands of miles away, at a distance of centuries from my cell—

this allowed me to forget my body. I felt it, I touched it, but gradually I managed to separate myself from it. By concentrating I would see myself calmly seated, back hunched, ribs sticking out, bent knees looking like two sharp points; I would observe myself, and I was a spirit hovering over the hole. I was not always able to manage this. The effort of concentration did not automatically lead to this detachment. It all depended on the heat and the cold. I knew that physical conditions competed with the desire to think myself out of that hell. Hell was not an image, a word uttered to exorcise misfortune. Hell was in us and around us. It was even useful to us: it allowed us to measure our strength, our ability to resist and to imagine another world—an immaterial one—where we could hide while a fresh wound was added to the barely dried blood of other injuries.

The days and nights were what we possessed in this hell. We were days of hunger and nights without sleep. Often we were nothing else. So those who took their own lives were ending their days and their nights. They had no pitiful illusions. Or else, what led them to suicide was precisely the poison of illusions. I realized that dignity was also the refusal to have anything more to do with hope. To survive you had to give up hope. The advantage of this conviction was that it had no connection with those who had thrown us in prison. It depended not on their strategy, but simply on our will: to break that insane habit of living in hope . . .

Hope was a complete denial of reality. How could these men abandoned by everyone be made to believe that this hole was only a parenthesis in their lives, that this ordeal would have an end, and that they would emerge from it stronger, better men? Hope was a lie with sedative properties. To overcome it we had to prepare for the worst every day. Those who did not understand this sank into a violent and fatal despair.

10

My gall bladder has gone crazy. It produces too much bile, flooding me with this bitter liquid. I am saturated with bile. Everything about me smells bitter. My mouth is dry and coated with bitterness. My tongue is heavy, my saliva is gummy. I see myself drowning in a vat of bile. I plunge in, held down by unknown hands. My head fills with greenish phlegm. When my nostrils clog up, I make myself sneeze. I strain to expel all this mucus, but my muscles are stiff. My joints are rigid and feel as if someone has tied them so they cannot move. They are useless. My hands have curled up and my fingers look like fishhooks. I can feel the liquid rising and falling throughout my body. My skin hurts. For a moment I think that the bile has solidified and is moving around in my stomach, tearing it like barbed wire.

Pain gives me an eerie lucidity. I suffer, but I know how to put a stop to this business. I must vomit, empty out that bile attacking all my organs. To do this, I must put my fingers in my mouth, press down on my tongue, and throw up. When you are healthy, this is childishly simple. But when your body is paralyzed with pain, any movement is a struggle. I am sitting with my head and back against the wall. My right arm is immobilized. It sticks to the wall as if glued there. I must slowly pry it loose and raise it to my mouth. Easy to say, extremely hard to do. I focus all my attention on my arm. My entire body is in this arm. I am an arm sitting on the floor, and I must push with all my strength to get up. Staring at the arm, I can forget the bitter taste in my mouth and even reduce the pain in my joints to faint twinges. I hear the pain echoing. I can feel it moving away, but not disappearing. I bend my head down to bring it closer to my hand. I feel the bile rising until it almost chokes me. I lean back quickly, whacking my skull against the wall. Holding my head still, I change tactics: my hand will come to my mouth, not vice versa. It takes hours. I use my other arm for support. I am bathed in sweat. Drops fall on my hand. What is most important is not to move, or think about anything but lifting that arm. I imagine a tiny crane descending from the roof, grasping my hand, and carrying it with precision to my mouth. I look up at the ceiling: nothing there. In the darkness, I manage not to see but at least to guess where things might be.

Time is meaningless now. It seems to pass particularly slowly and serves, apparently, to paralyze the arms and hands. After several hours, when I succeed in putting my fingers inside my mouth, I stop a moment to savor my little victory. Then I press on my tongue, but the bile does not come up right away. When the first stream gushes out over my hands, feet, and the floor, I quiver with relief. Pressing down again, I vomit with still more force. I have become a fountain of bile. My throat is irritated, my eyes bulge from their sockets, and tears streak my cheeks. I am rid of the poison that burned my esophagus.

I feel light, famished, and prepare to attain ecstasy, that state in which nothing holds me back with any connection to either beings or objects. I leave everything behind, abandoning myself and my companions, who have no idea of the anguish I have just gone through. I am in superb solitude, where only the breeze can still waft across the terraces of my isolation. And then I experience a dazzling amazement, followed by great fatigue. There I am inaccessible. I fly like a joyous bird. I don't stray too far from where I have left my body, for fear they might take it away and bury it. The body is breathing quite slowly, it's true, and does seem to be dead or in a coma.

The instant I realized that my cell stank to high heaven, I knew I had returned to my body. The state of grace was over. Once more I prepared to deal with my usual problems. I stood up and poured the rest of my water supply on the floor. That night, I slept standing. The cold rose from the soles of my feet right up to my skull, taking its time, lingering a good while at my belly, where it left a little of its arrogance, hatred, and contempt. For me, cold had a face, hands—or rather, pinching claws. It bit my testicles. I bent over, the better to endure its bite. The cold strolled up and down my body, making it shiver. I shuffled over the damp ground. I could not let the cold win. I returned to my exercises, mentally saying my daily prayers.

There are five prayers every good Muslim should recite. I was not clean. Not enough water for my ablutions. I prayed silently, invoking a superior force, the force of justice, Allah and His prophets, the sea and the sky, the mountains and the prairies.

"Save me from hatred, that destructive impulse, the poison that ravages the heart and liver. I must stop wanting to take revenge on other lives, on other minds; I must forget hatred, reject it, refuse to answer it with more hatred. I must rise above it. Help me to renounce this crippling bond, to leave without hindrance this body that no longer looks like one, but like a jumble of deformed bones; direct my eyes to other stones. This darkness suits me: when I look inside myself, I see more clearly through the confusion of my situation. I am no longer of this world, even if my feet are still freezing on this damp cement floor. The back of my neck hurts because I cannot stand up straight. No—I feel no pain. I am certain that I feel no pain. I do not feel anything anymore. My prayer has been answered. I am not ill. I never will be, here, no matter how I suffer. O my God, I have learned from You that a healthy body teaches us about the beauty of the world. It is the echo of enchantment, produced by life and light. It is light. Light in life. When it is withdrawn from life, isolated and imprisoned in a black hole, it no longer echoes anything, it reflects nothing. Thanks to Your will, I shall never be extinguished."

11

A sliver of sky must have hovered right above the vent, the indirect opening that let in air but no light. I sensed the presence of this sky, and filled it with words and images. I shifted the stars around, meddling with them to make room for a little of that light imprisoned in my breast. I felt that radiance. How can one feel light? When an inner brightness caressed my skin and warmed it, I knew that it was visiting me. I could not manage to make it stay. Instead, there was silence. It would fall suddenly on our blind eyes. It enveloped us, alighting like a calming hand upon our shoulders. Even when it was heavy, still laden with dust, it did me good. It never weighed on me. I should say that there were different kinds of silence.

The silence of night. It was a necessity for us.

The silence of the companion who was slowly leaving us.

The silence we observed as a sign of mourning.

The silence of blood circulating sluggishly.

The silence that told us where the scorpions were.

The silence of images we ran and reran through our minds.

The silence of the guards that expressed weariness and routine.

The silence of the shadow of memories burned to ashes.

The silence of a leaden sky from which almost no sign could reach us.

The silence of absence, the blinding absence of life.

The hardest, most unbearable silence was that of light. A powerful and manifold silence. There was the silence of the night, always the same, and then there were the silences of light. A long and endless absence.

Outside, not only over our pit but above all far away from it, there was life. You could not think too much about it, but I liked to imagine it so as not to die of forgetfulness. Imagine, and not remember. Life, the real one, not that dirty rag blowing across the ground, no, life in its exquisite beauty, I mean in its simplicity, its marvelous banality: a child smiling after tears; eyes blinking in too bright a light; a woman trying on a dress; a man asleep on the grass. A horse galloping across a plain. A man wearing many-colored wings attempting to fly. A tree bending down to shade a woman sitting on a stone. The sun drifts off, and you even see a rainbow. Life: it's being able to raise your arm, rub the back of your neck, stretch for the pure pleasure of it, get up and stroll along aimlessly, watch people go by, stop, read a newspaper—or simply stay sitting at your window because you have nothing to do and it's nice to do nothing.

I imagined that the clamor of life was a kaleidoscope of all colors, that it made noise as it breezed through the trees. This escape was not meant to last a long while. A little indulgence to prepare me for more demanding concentration.

Even dead, or more exactly, considered as such by my family, I had to make the journey home. Without nostalgia. Without emotion.

How to reassure my mother, tell her that I am fighting, resisting? How to let her know that this will to hold my head high and remain dignified—this willpower comes from her? I had confidence in her intuitions. So, mentally, I spoke to her, in a letter I would perhaps write one day, on paper, with a pencil, a letter that would reach her by messenger or even through the mail.

"Dearest Yamma, my darling Moumti, I kiss your hands and lay my head on your shoulder. I am in good health, don't worry. I believe you can be proud of me. I am a credit to you. Not only am I resisting, but I help the others to endure the unbearable. I won't tell you how they treat us. I work hard at forgetting. I know that you have trouble falling asleep, that you climb up and down the same mountain. Take care of your heart, don't forget your medications. Be calm, there's no use in you upsetting yourself. I'm going through a long tunnel. I keep walking and I'm sure that some day, when I reach the end, I will see the light; it will have to be soft, because too strong a brightness would blind me. You will be there waiting for me, you will bring me bread made with your own hands, warm bread dipped in oil from the seeds of the argan tree. That is all I will eat for several days, to let my stomach get used to receiving something besides starchy foods. You will come with a woolen blanket, and you will wrap me up in it like a baby, like you used to when I was a child; I have grown light, you will take me in your arms and you will sing me Grandmother's counting rhyme.

"The farther I go, the more confident I am. I pray, I talk to God, I dream of the black stone, and sometimes I leave my body and see myself from the outside. I admit that it is most difficult to achieve this serenity. That, too, I have learned from you. You remember, when my father used to wound you, wasting all the household money, you would gather us together, and without speaking ill of that man in any way, you would make us responsible for ourselves. His rages, his injustices would not touch you. You were above that. I admired you, because you always kept your composure. The only times you lost your head were when your last little one, your 'lambkin,' would run away. You'd tell us, 'You are all my children, but he, he is my eyes, my very breath.' And he adored you, too. I remember the day he came home from school, tossed down his book bag, and went looking for you in the kitchen the way he always did. The maid told him that you had gone to Rabat to take care of an administrative problem. Unable to bear your absence, he shut himself up in the wardrobe where your dresses were hanging. He smelled your odor, your perfume clinging to your clothes. Shut up like that, in tears, he began to run a temperature. When you came home, late that evening, you went straight to the wardrobe and found him burning up with fever. He was writhing in pain. It was an attack of appendicitis. You spent the night in the emergency room, and you went back to work the next morning without a wink of sleep. The operation was a success and all was well again.

"Oh, Mama, I must confess I found it hard to put up with the way you fed him. You would chew the meat, roll it in the palm of your hand, and pop it into his mouth. And he, like a chick, beak gaping, gobbled up his food. He laughed, making fun of us, while you, lost in happiness, said nothing. We laughed, too, making fun of both of you. You showered that child with all the love you had never been given. We were kids, we didn't understand that.

"Our father made several attempts to win you back. He would come, preceded by *mokhaznis,* former servants at the court of Pasha El Glaoui, their hands filled with gifts, magnificent fabrics imported from Europe, trays heaped with sugarloaves. He arrived as if he were asking for you in marriage for the first time. Coming forward, hands behind his back, he would beg you to forgive him. You wouldn't unbolt the door, and from a half-opened window, you ordered the *mokhaznis* to go carry all those things to the second wife's house. He had married again without your knowledge, while you slaved, alone, without help, with little means of support.

"You were admirable. You resolutely sent that man away. You never weakened or gave in. Your strength of character was your freedom. Your determination to live with dignity made you stronger, more beautiful. I was the eldest son, and as soon as I could, I left home to lighten your burden. I joined the army, not because I loved it, but because it guaranteed me a salary, training, bed and board. I insisted on sending you a good part of my pay. I did so gladly, because I knew you needed it, while I could live with very little money.

"My father did not even know that I had entered the Military Academy. He was already at the palace, making life more pleasant for his king. The palace took care of his second wife, their children, and their house. I saw my father only on television, when royal activities were broadcast. He would stand in the background, looking important and alert. This gifted scholar, with his phenomenal memory, had become a buffoon, a mountebank, a jester, a professional entertainer at the court of the most powerful man in the country. For although he didn't make us laugh, our father had a wonderful sense of humor. At home he was always just passing through. He was famous for his intelligence and his gift for repartee. He was a walking library. I would admire him when he recited poems to his friends. He never made mistakes. And he also knew everything there was to know about gold and traditional jewelry. But that man was a bad husband and an absent father, or simply too preoccupied with himself, with his taste for girls—those younger than twenty—and his love of elegant clothes, his need for festivity, for pleasure and good times. He took everything lightly and could not stand to be alone.

"Oh, Mama, I feel that you are sad. Tell yourself that I'm traveling, discovering an unfathomable world, discovering myself, learning with each passing day what you've made of me. I thank you. I kiss your hands, I'm deeply sorry for the pain I've caused you by my involvement in this affair. But, as you can guess, no one consulted the cadets and junior officers about it. We definitely suspected something was going on, but, like good soldiers, we followed our leaders. To you I can say this and know that you will believe me: I did not kill anyone. I never fired a single shot. I was in a complete panic. I aimed my gun at people. I admit I was looking for my father. I'll never know whether it was to save him from that massacre or to shoot him. This question haunts me. Torments me. If I repeat myself, it's because I'm forced to go around in circles.

"Dear Mama, I must leave you. I hear cries of pain . . ."

Mustapha, cell number 8, was screaming. Had he been stung by a scorpion? In his agony he kept getting up and then collapsing back onto the cement. The pain was growing worse. It was the middle of the night, so we could not call the guards to let in Wakrine, our venom-sucking specialist, to help him. Awakened by the cries, Karim told us the time: "It's 3:16 in the morning on Thursday, April 25, 1979."

Weeping, Mustapha yelled, "I want to die, but not like this, not from a scorpion sting! No—if I have to die, I'll be the one to decide! No, no, poison is a terrible thing, I can't breathe, I'm suffocating, dizzy, I'm dying . . . Oh my God, why now? Why in the dead of night?"

Wakrine told him to hold on until the guards brought our breakfast coffee. They would have to let Wakrine save him.

Poor Mustapha did his best. He lost consciousness. We thought he was gone; Gharbi even began to recite the Koran for him. We all joined in. Mustapha gave a loud cry—then nothing more.

When the guards arrived in the morning, we began reciting the Koran again. They allowed Wakrine to go to cell 8. He staggered back in revulsion. All the scorpions in the dungeon were on Mustapha's decomposing body. Clapping our hands and stamping our feet, we called for the Kmandar. These deadly creatures had to be exterminated.

"Kmandar, Kmandar, Kmandar . . ."

There was nothing Wakrine could do for poor Mustapha, a quiet fellow with whom we played cards. He was an excellent player, and understood better than any of us how one could amuse oneself simply through imagination. We had no cards, of course, but Bourras, Number 13, dealt out make-believe ones. Four of us would get together, and we invented a game with face-up cards: matching numbers with spades while we told stories.

The Kmandar did not appear, but the guards took action, hunting down the scorpions while we washed Mustapha's corpse in his cell.

As we were bringing out the body, the guards arrived with strips of black cloth: "You can only come outside blindfolded!" Someone protested; they locked him back up in his cell.

Six months had passed since the last funeral. We could hardly walk. This time, the daylight was filtered by the black bands. My eyes, my scalp, my skin hurt . . . My whole body ached. We shuffled forward. Moh, Number 1, bent down to pick up something from the ground and swallowed it. A guard saw him and threatened him with his weapon.

"Spit out that grass you ate or I'll waste you!"

It was too late. Moh laughed. The angry guard grabbed him by the back of the neck and threw him down. Another guard intervened, preventing him from shooting.

After that incident, we had ten minutes to lay Mustapha in his grave. When a guard brought the bucket of quicklime and poured it over the body, Moh jumped into the grave, determined to end it all. We managed to get him out of there—he just had a little quicklime on his feet. The commotion brought the head guard over in a hurry. We could hear him coming, cursing life and the fate that had sent him to this godforsaken place.

"This is the last time outside for you. No more funerals. That's it! Finished! You will no longer leave your cells. The only way you'll get out will be eyes closed, feet first, in a plastic bag. I almost landed in prison because of you! In Rabat, headquarters is furious. You'll never get outside again. Never! Ever! You're condemned to eternal darkness. No more light for you. The orders are categorical: darkness, dry bread, and water. All right, clear out of here! Oh my God, what did I do that was so terrible I had to get sent to this hell? And yet I say my prayers, fast during Ramadan, give to charity . . . So why make me the shepherd for this flock of lost souls?"

From that day on, Moh slowly went mad. We would hear him talking to his mother at meal times.

"Ma, Yamma, it's ready, come eat . . . Ah! You can't move. I'm coming, I'm bringing you a tray. I've made you the *tanjia* you love. Today, we're not dieting. The meat is quite tender. I cooked it over charcoal. It's real *tanjia marrakchie:* * lamb, olive oil, pepper, salt, ginger, and preserved lemon. Braised, it's excellent. Not very greasy. You know, before I put the meat in the *tanjia,* I trimmed the fat. We treat lamb and mutton as though they were the same—well, I can guarantee you this is lamb. Have some bread. Oh, no bread? Ah, the diabetes! You smell how good the stew is? All right, no vegetables. No starches: too fattening. Ma, don't bother, open your mouth. I know, your eyesight's getting so bad, it's all on account of that damned sugar! There, I've picked out a very tender piece. Eat, take your time chewing. Ah, you want something to drink, you've got the hiccups. Oh dear! My mother has the hiccups. Friends, what should I do? My mother's having trouble breathing, help me . . . Here, drink this, it's sparkling water. You like that. Water with bubbles. Oof! All better now. You know, Mama, they worry me, your hiccups. It's like death knocking at the door. Father died because he swallowed something that went down the wrong way. Here, another mouthful. Slowly . . . Ah, the lemon's too salty. Let's take out the lemon. Oh, you'd like a piece of eggplant? But Mama, there isn't any eggplant in the *tanjia*. Have you forgotten? It was even you who taught me how to make it. Come on, eat. Here, have a bite more meat. No, open your mouth, I can use my fork. There. It's good. You're ashamed to be fed like a baby? But Mama, the paralysis has reached your arm. You can't eat on your own. Luckily, I'm here. It's my duty to help you and feed you. That's what children are for. I'm your last little one. I'm more attentive than the others. But they do what they can. Me, I have all the time in the world. I have nothing to do. I don't work anymore. I'm on leave. The army no longer needs us. There are a few of us spending our vacation away from the barracks. I've plenty of time, that's how come I was able to fix you the *tanjia* you like so much. You're not hungry anymore. Ah! You want to feed me? No, not hungry. I'd like to nurse, yes, *ya Yamma,* give me your breast. I need your breast so much, let me lay my head on that breast, while your fingers stroke my hair . . . Forgive me, your hands can't move, and I have no hair anymore. I'll leave you, now. For this evening, I'm planning a light supper: artichokes— you know, the little ones with the sharp leaves, boiled in water, with a bowl of milk curds and an apple. One should eat spar-

ingly in the evening, to avoid spending a difficult night. Now
I'll go do the dishes. No doubt about it, Moroccan lamb is too
fatty. That's the last time I'll make a *tanjia!*"

Poor Moh had us in stitches at every mealtime. We let him talk.
It was his way of unwinding. And we would get these cravings
... That was dangerous. We couldn't think about food anymore. We had finally gotten used to the tasteless starches and
stale bread. Moh had obviously been a good cook back in
Ahermemou, and his words made our mouths water. I wanted
to make him be quiet, but I had no right to do that. He was losing his mind. He was feeding an imaginary mother while he
himself had stopped eating.

"Mama," he said another day, "I didn't find any meat or vegetables in the market this morning. The market is gone. It's been
moved. I got out my bike, but kids had let the air out of the tires.
All I found were starchy things: white beans, chickpeas, dried
fava beans. The bread is stale, hard, it has to be soaked in water
or it's inedible. You tell me you're not hungry. You're right. Me
neither—I'm never hungry anymore. I no longer feel like cook-
ing now. You think you'd like some grilled sardines sprinkled
with onions and parsley. That's a good idea. But it's oily, Mama.
You'll get heartburn. No, I'd suggest boiled mackerel with a few
potatoes. No—not boiled: in a *tanjia,* with tomatoes, onions, a
sauce with cumin, red pepper, a bit spicy, with some coriander, a
few garlic cloves, and you let it simmer over a low flame. So, I'm
off to the harbor to buy what we need, the boats are coming in.
I'll check with Abdeslam, our fisherman cousin. Oh, no sea
bream, too many bones. You're right. Father almost died swallowing a fishbone. Ah! That's true, it did kill him. I'd forgotten.
Forgive me, Mama. Well, I have to get going. But don't ask me
again where I'm off to, you know that on Fridays I always take
couscous* to the poor outside the mosque. Today's Friday. Oh!
You forgot the charity meal, you didn't make the couscous.

They're not going to be very happy, all those poor people waiting for me. I won't go to the mosque. I'll say my prayers at
home . . ."

As time went by, his voice grew fainter. He mumbled, muttered,
ground his teeth, sighed. Uneaten meals piled up in his cell and
rotted. He wasn't bathing anymore. With his long, long nails,
he scratched at the wall. He had no more strength, no more
voice. He was letting himself die, since he had stopped eating
quite a while ago and was not feeding his mother now. It took
him several weeks to pass away.

12

Laughter. We tried to laugh by telling old jokes. Our merriment was often forced, a kind of nervous stutter. The laughter of despair has a color, an odor, and our gaiety made us even more miserable. Ours made us even more miserable. Mustapha came up with puns, witticisms, gave everyone nicknames. It was sometimes amusing. But we missed beautiful, honest, scandalous, ringing laughter, the laughter of life, pleasure, health, and confident well-being. And yet, we could have laughed like that if we had reached a deeper understanding of our plight. But we did not all have the same needs or the same will to resist.

Laughter, the uproarious kind, that just bursts out and does one good—it would be the Kmandar who provoked it. That Kmandar we had never seen was quite a presence in our darkness. The guards kept us informed of his orders and whims. One day, M'Fadel charged into the building raving and cursing the animal kingdom and dogs in particular.

"God damn the religion of dogs and the religion of doglovers, who adopt them and let them sleep in their own beds! May God get rid of the canine race and all its descendants, may He put them in a huge cauldron so they won't reproduce ever again or come pestering us out in this forlorn dump in our beloved country! Go on, get moving, you'll share the fate of those who tried to kill Sidna!* Hurry up, you bastard, you're going to croak, you'll get hydrophobia, and then I'll throw you myself into the boiling cauldron. I'm obeying the Kmandar for now, I'm imprisoning you with the others. You'll be locked up and you'll eat only once a day, noodles cooked in water!"

We were flabbergasted. A dog condemned to five years in jail! That's a life sentence! It seemed he had bitten a general who had arrived to inspect the barracks near the prison.

After that, laughter came back to us.

Our daily life experienced a slight disruption. Some of us were angry at being imprisoned along with a dog. Others looked on the good side of this business. We decided to give him a name, but could not decide which one.

"Me, I say call him Kmandar!"

"No, I'm sure this dog is more human than the Kmandar."

"So we'll call him Tony!"

"But why Tony? That's a man's name."

"No reason—because it sounds Italian, snazzy . . . and also it rhymes with bony."

"No, we'll just call him the Kelb.* Kelb or Kleb, as the French say."

"And why not Ditto?"

"You mean he's like us?"

"Yes and no. Who cares!"

"Ditto it is. Vote on it?"

"Okay. Let's vote."

And so the dog was named Ditto and became a not insignificant member of our group.

We got used to him. He never bellyached. Sometimes we heard him going round and round in his cell, thwacking the door with his tail. Hunger and thirst made him mean. He did not bark, but whimpered, as if he were wounded. Obviously, he relieved himself all over the cell. The excrement piled up and the stench was pervasive. We had to do something, move him elsewhere, tie him up in a forest, or find him a separate prison. M'Fadel agreed, but he could not speak to the Kmandar about it.

After a month Ditto went mad, probably from rabies. His howls became more and more unbearable. The guards no longer dared open his cell door to give him food. He died of hunger and exhaustion. His carcass stank. We made no more jokes; we just didn't have the heart.

*   *   *

To resist, you must think. Without consciousness, without thought, there is no resistance. In the end we no longer felt like laughing at the Kmandar's cruelty. Ditto was carried off in a wheelbarrow. We were relieved. His cell had to be cleaned and disinfected. The guards waited a week before doing this. Apparently, they were embarrassed by this delay, because M'Fadel told us, between two groans, "Kmandar's orders!"

After this episode—more grotesque than comic—I went back to praying and meditating in the silence of the night. I invoked God by His many names. I gently left my cell and no longer felt the ground. I withdrew from everything until all I saw of my body was its translucent exterior. I was naked. Nothing to hide. Nothing to show. From this darkness the truth appeared to me in its dazzling light. I was nothing. Nothing but a grain of wheat beneath a vast millstone that slowly crushed us one by one. I thought once again about the Sura of Light and heard myself repeat the verse, "You see how powerful is the darkness of this light. Stretch out your hand, and you will not even see it."

I reflected and understood that veils were falling, one after another, and that the darkness had become less opaque, pierced by the faintest ray of light. Perhaps I was inventing it, imagining it. I convinced myself that I was seeing it. The silence was a path, a way to return to myself. I was silence. My breathing, my heartbeats became silence. My inner nakedness was my secret. There was no need for me to exhibit or celebrate it in that small lonely place smelling of mildew and urine. After some time of great lucidity, I fell back under the millstone turning slowly, slowly . . .

13

He was an adjutant, a simple adjutant, but also the most powerful noncommissioned officer in Ahermemou, the right-hand man of Commandant A. Tall, strong, with deep-set eyes, a direct gaze, he had served in Indochina. His name was Atta. A Berber, a man of the plains, someone from nowhere. He was married and probably had kids, but nothing about him gave any clues to his family life. He seemed to have no family, no friends. A man of steely strictness and discipline. He was feared and respected. He spoke very little and had one of the loudest voices in the camp. With his shaved skull, he looked like the American TV detective Kojak. We knew that he was more important than all the officers in the academy, that he and the commandant had a pact, a secret bond, something that baffled us and that we did not even try to understand.

He was the one who drove us to the palace. The commandant was ahead of us. We did not see him. Atta was in radio contact with him. After the massacre in Skhirate, Atta disappeared. Most of the officers had been killed. He had fled. It seems someone saw him running inside the palace.

When I got out of the hole, I learned what had happened. Atta had in fact rushed into one of the rooms in the palace, looking not for the king but for two of our companions, two cadets who had gone off on their own beyond the swimming pool area. He found them in a room, probably part of the royal apartments, terrorizing a woman: one of them was holding her down on the floor and forcing her legs open, while the other was trying to stick the muzzle of his rifle into her vagina. Red-eyed with fury, the cadet trying to rape her with his gun was shouting, "Where he sticks his dick, I'm sticking my rifle!"

Atta came up behind them and shouted, *"Balkoum!"* ("Attention!") The two cadets sprang automatically to attention.

Atta ordered them to leave the palace, and apologized to the woman, who was half unconscious. Then he left through the kitchens opening out onto the beach.

The two cadets were arrested at the entrance to the golf course; Atta was only caught several days later.

He was in our group. During the first few months he did not say one word. His attitude was perfectly clear: "I lost, I pay."

One day, the guards came for him. He followed them. Before leaving the pit, he said to us in French, *"Adieu!"*

"Adieu!" we all called after him.

We thought his time had come. Summary execution or endless sessions of torture. We had no way of knowing. As for us, we figured they were going to kill us one by one, and that he was at the top of the list.

Later I would find out, from someone who was there, that his story was more complicated than we thought. They blindfolded him and took him to a house where he was ordered to bathe, shave, and put on clean clothes. That evening they served him a real supper. He ate only bread. He knew that he should not eat too much after months of living on nothing but starchy food. There was a bed; he chose to sleep on the floor. The next day, he asked permission to say his prayers, dressed, and announced, "I'm ready to go to God."

Nothing else was said. Other soldiers came on duty, commanded by a young captain. They took Atta back to Skhirate, hands cuffed behind his back, a black jute sack over his head. He was as closely guarded as if they had feared an attempt on his life. He walked with his head held high, asking no questions, showing no apprehension about what he suspected would happen.

Other guards took over and led him through the palace to the room where he had saved the woman who was being raped. Nothing had changed. Same décor, same rug, same black leather sofa. He stood there the entire day. They removed the black bag and blindfolded him. At night they brought him food. He asked the guards to change his handcuffs to the front. After consulting with their captain, they did. It was just so that he could feed himself. He took only bread and water. He stretched out on the rug while the guards kept watch. He motioned for them to cuff his hands behind his back again. Another consultation. Request granted.

He did not really sleep. At around two in the morning, the captain came to get him. They left the room. Armed guards stayed close to him. Counter-order. He was returned to the room. When the captain removed the blindfold and handcuffs, Atta found himself standing before the king, about thirty feet away. Saluting, he snapped to attention, and since the king did not order him to stand at ease, Atta remained stiffly at attention throughout their interview.

"Do you know why I have brought you here?"

"No, Majesty."

"Do you remember what happened in this room?"

Atta pretended to consider the question.

"Yes, Majesty."

"I want the names of the two animals you found here."

Atta never wavered. Silence.

"Answer His Majesty," the captain ordered.

Silence.

"If you give me the names of those two individuals, tonight you will be home with your children. You have my word."

"I am sorry, Majesty. I do not know their names."

"You're sure?"

"Yes, Majesty."

"You don't want to save your life. Too bad."

The king vanished, followed by his aides-de-camp.

The guards surrounded Atta. The captain blindfolded him. He pulled the cloth very tight, as if in anger. He placed the black jute bag over his head again and handcuffed him. Atta did not flinch. He stood ramrod-straight, ready to be executed or returned to prison.

The captain murmured to him, "Why are you protecting those two pigs?"

Atta said nothing.

He was taken away in the middle of the night. They say he was shot while attempting to escape. All anyone knows, even today, is that he did not return to Tazmamart, and that he is dead.

14

If Gharbi's mission was to recite the Koran aloud in certain circumstances, if Karim was chosen as the guardian of time (we called him the calendar or the talking clock), if Wakrine was the scorpion specialist, then I was the storyteller. My companions unanimously elected me to the post, perhaps because some of them knew that my father was a teller of riddles and tales, or simply because they had heard me reciting poems by Ahmed Chawqui,* called "the prince of poets." I knew *The Flowers of Evil* and *The Little Prince* by heart, but they wanted to hear the *Thousand and One Nights,* which I had not read, although I was familiar with certain of its episodes attributed to Jha, also called Goha.

I explained repeatedly to my companions that I did not know the book, but they did not believe me and kept pleading for its stories. Abdelkader, Number 2, was a shy little man who often spoke almost in a whisper.

"Tell me a story," he begged me, "or I'll die . . ."

"But Kader, really, no story I could tell you would give you the strength you need to live and bear up under everything they do to us."

"Oh yes it would. I need words, I dream of hearing them, of welcoming them inside my head, of dressing them in images, making them spin like a merry-go-round, keeping them warm, and showing this film when I'm in pain, when I'm afraid of going crazy. Come on, don't be stingy, open up, talk, tell a story, make it up if you want, but give us a bit of your imagination."

I was truly sorry not to have read *The Arabian Nights.* It was a question of chance: you tell yourself you have plenty of time, you save a few books for later . . . and forget to read them. My father had a vast library. A large section was reserved for Arab manuscripts, which he collected, while the rest housed works in

French and English. Even if he did not read all these books, he loved to buy them and arrange them on his shelves. He had them rebound and sorted them by subject. My mother objected, because she did not have money for our schoolbooks, while my father was off rummaging through bookstores after some old manuscript for which he would often pay an extravagant price. But living surrounded by books turned out to be important in our education. All my brothers and sisters love books and reading.

After lunch—well, after our midday starches—complete silence fell. I sensed everyone's anticipation. I plunged in without knowing what I was going to say or how the tale would end.

"Once upon a time there was a rich man, so rich he had no idea how vast his fortune was. But he was an incredible miser. Although he had two wives, neither of them had managed to give him a child."

From the far end of the cell block a voice cried out, "Hey! Describe the women for us. I want to know if they were blondes or brunettes, fat or slim, virtuous or lascivious . . ."

"They were as you like them: beautiful and sensual, submissive and cunning, depraved and amoral, intelligent and naive, lovely to caress, delightfully fragrant, cruel when abandoned, always mysterious. There you have it: this wealthy man's wives had every endearing quality and at the same time could be formidable indeed. The one was a plump brunette with hair so long it clothed her down to her knees. She had big breasts, too big for her little hands to hold. When she lay on her back, her breasts overflowed down her sides. Her eyes were the black color of ripe cherries, and the look in them could be daunting— people said it knocked birds right out of the sky. The other wife was a slender redhead. Her freckles made her even more desirable. Her bust was neither large nor small. She loved to oil her skin and massage her master while straddling him. Her eyes changed color with the light and the seasons. Sometimes they were light brown, sometimes they were flecked with violet and green. May I continue? So, I was saying that our man had a problem. He was sterile. He consulted doctors throughout the world, but it was no use. They all made the same diagnosis: sterility.

"As time passed, in spite of his gold and silver, he grew bored. His obsession with having an heir made him crazy and mistrustful. He became convinced that one of his wives had cast an evil spell on him . . ."

Kader interrupted to request an elaborate description of the rich man's palaces. That was easy. I piled on the details and invented a fantastic world.

"You know, more than anything else, a palace is a place where you feel a sense of well-being, where your body and soul are in harmony, where the real treasure is serenity. The rest is just decoration, space furnished according to your personal idea of contentment. Obviously, there's considerable comfort, but tell yourself one thing: real comfort comes from inner peace. It isn't Chinese or Persian carpets, Italian marble, or Bohemian crystal chandeliers that bring beauty and happiness. Let's say, to humor you, that our rich man has built an immense palace to display the tokens of his fortune. But despite the silk and crystal, the fountains and gardens, the slaves at his beck and call, he wasn't happy. You see, he had everything, except one thing that billions of men possess: the ability to get a woman with child."

Then I picked up the thread of my story, which ended three days later with the following moral.

"A miser is someone who keeps a tight hold on everything: money, time, emotions. He does not give. He does not give anything. Therefore he cannot give his wife the seed that would bring life!"

*   *   *

Now that I was a storyteller, I went back and forth between tales and poems. On one day, I would conjure up an unbelievable story, exaggerating wildly to keep my audience from bumping into the life they had left behind. I felt it was essential not to provide any historical or geographical reference points. Often the action unfolded in the vague past of a mythical Orient, as chaotic and far away as possible.

The next day, I would recite poems. I could not hope to match my father, with his extraordinary repertoire, but I have an excellent memory. So does my younger sister—we used to have poetry contests, sometimes in French, sometimes in Arabic.

Reciting the opening pages of *Uninterrupted Poetry* by Paul Éluard, I faltered at this stanza, tripping over certain words.

Today the one and only light
Today (. . . life . . . no) childhood whole
Changing life into light
With no past no tomorrow
Today dream of night
In broad day all breaks (. . . down . . . no) free
Today I am still and always

I repeated the stanza several times, as if I were getting stuck on the reference to that light so cruelly denied us. I hammered out each verse like a cranky old schoolteacher on the verge of losing his memory. "With no past no tomorrow," the others parroted after me, some of them speaking in Arabic: *"Bila mâdi bila ghad."* It was enough to put us all in a trance, possessed as we were by these words we had claimed for ourselves, convinced they had been written for us. I went back to an earlier part of the poem and began again.

Nothing can disturb the order of light
Where I am only myself
And what I love . . .

"That's wrong!" screamed a voice. "*They* have dared to upset and destroy the order of light! In our country they don't respect light, or day, or night, or children, or women, or my poor mother who must have died from waiting for a missing son to come home . . . No, they've ground light into the dirt!"

To put an end to this disturbance, Gharbi intoned the call to prayer. Then all was silent again.

So I think that I and Karim, our faithful watchman of Time, were the two busiest convicts in our group. I kept trying to come up with stories. It was not enough to remember those I had been told when I was a kid: I had to elaborate, invent, digress, pause for a moment and ask questions. Difficult craft, fascinating work.

After the tales and poems, I moved on to films. I rehashed the plots of the ones I had seen in Marrakech during the period when I was going to the movies every day. I had a passion for them. I even planned to become a producer. I had my preferences, my favorites. I was partial to American films from the forties and fifties. I felt that black and white gave these stories a dramatic impact that transported us far away from banal reality.

"My friends, I would like your attention and absolute quiet, because I'm going to take you to America in the 1950s. The scene is in black and white. The film is called *A Streetcar Named Desire;* it's the streetcar that a young woman, Blanche DuBois, takes when she arrives in New Orleans to visit her sister Stella, who is married to Marlon Brando in the role of Stanley, a working man of Polish background. As you know, America is made up of immigrants from all over the world.

"What's Stella like? She's a happy, healthy young woman. She and her husband live modestly in a poor neighborhood in New Orleans. As for Blanche, she's not in great shape. I must add that her husband committed suicide some time earlier."

"Why?" someone shouted.

"Listen, that's not important, the main thing is that this woman arrives at her sister's place and turns it upside down because she's been knocked for a loop by the sudden loss of her husband."

"And Marlon Brando, what's he like?"

"He's young and handsome. He wears a white T-shirt. He's often in a bad mood, particularly since the arrival of his sister-in-law. I'd like to point out one detail: after the streetcar Desire, Blanche takes another called Cemetery, and gets off at the Elysian Fields stop."

"Is Brando going to make a pass at his sister-in-law?"

"No. Blanche is fragile. She's got psychological problems. She claims that financial difficulties have forced her to sell the family home. She's lying. First she'll say one thing and then exactly the opposite."

"You mean she wanders in and out of her words?"

"That's right. She's not in control of what she says. Stanley discovers she has money and jewelry in her suitcase. That's a lot for a simple schoolteacher. So he asks someone to investigate what Blanche was up to before she came to stay with them."

"She must have been a whore!"

"Don't rush things. For the moment, imagine a table at which Stanley and his friends, including Mitch, are playing cards. They're smoking, drinking beer, laughing, telling jokes. Blanche appears, lovely, dressed in white. Mitch turns his head. He forgets the poker game. The camera follows his gaze. Blanche walks by once, twice. It's love at first sight. The camera returns to Marlon Brando. You can see from his face he's not pleased. The music underscores this. The card game is over and the men leave the table, but Stanley is angry. He drinks too much and gets violent. His T-shirt is damp with sweat. Close-up on the young Brando's back as he moves toward Blanche. His wife intervenes. He hits her, then tangles with Mitch. The two sisters take refuge with a woman friend. Now there's a beautiful movie scene: Brando is in the street, drunk, his clothes torn, howling his wife's name. Stella goes to join him. He falls to his knees, wraps his arms around her, and sobs into her skirt."

"Hey, Salim, that's not right! A man, a real one, doesn't throw himself at his wife's feet! You're making that up!"

"No, I'm not making anything up. The film script is taken from a play by Tennessee Williams."

"I don't know who he is! But where I come from, a woman who runs off has no right to come back and still less to have her man on his knees!"

"Well, this is in America. Okay! May I continue? Stella—I forgot to tell you—is pregnant. It's normal that a husband would be nice to his wife, especially after behaving like a brute!"

"And the investigation of Blanche? She's a whore, right?"

"We learn from the inquiry that her husband died young, that she had affairs with men who were just passing through town. Maybe she's been a prostitute off and on; in any case, she's a sick woman. She's a pathological liar."

"She's a what?"

"She lies constantly and believes her own lies."

"That's like Achar who thinks he killed fifteen Chinese in Indochina!"

"That has nothing to do with it. And besides, the people of Indochina are the Vietnamese. All right, let's get back to New Orleans. Stanley tells his friend Mitch the truth. Stella goes off to the hospital to have her baby. Stanley and Blanche find themselves alone, face-to-face. Very beautiful scene. Brando's going to tell poor Blanche what's what. They trade insults. The tension rises. Brando jumps her and rapes her. Blanche goes crazy. She raves and screams. A doctor and a nurse come to get her. Stella gives birth. She's in tears. She tells Stanley he'll never touch her again. She takes her baby and goes to stay with a neighbor lady. Stanley yells her name. From her room, she can hear his long, echoing cry. Blanche has been confined to an asylum. Mitch has lost his illusions, and the streetcar goes on carrying wounded souls through the city."

"That's it?"

"Yes, that's it."

"But why does Brando rape his sister-in-law?"

"Because she attracted and exasperated him. Rape is the expression of an imbalance, a maladjustment . . ."

With time, and the slow, steady deterioration of my mental as well as physical abilities, I could no longer keep my audience enthralled. My bones hurt. My spine ached because I slept hunched up. Through a protracted effort of concentration and detachment, I could overcome the pain, but it would become too much for me whenever I talked to my companions, because the process that let me be elsewhere had been interrupted. So I became a storyteller full of holes, no longer able to play my part. I needed to get a grip on myself, to isolate myself, in a way, even though we were all in complete isolation, prone to sickness and despair. Every day, Abdelkader would beg for stories.

"Salim, my friend, our man of letters blessed with a magnificent imagination, give me something to drink. To me, each sentence is a glass of pure water, spring water. I'll do without their beans and chickpeas, I'll share my ration of water with you, but please, tell me a story, a long and fantastic story. I need one. It's vital. It's my hope, my oxygen, my freedom. Salim, you who have read everything, you who remember all the verses, the commas and periods, you who re-create the other world where everything is possible—don't abandon me, don't forget me! My sickness can only be treated with words and images. Thanks to you, for a few moments I was Marlon Brando. In my head I walk the way he walks in films. In my head I look at women the way he looks at them in life. You gave me a gift. As soon as your story was over, I wasn't Marlon Brando anymore. I love your metaphors, I adore your irony, thanks to you I can forget my bruised body and go traveling. I fly, I stroll, I see the stars and I no longer feel the pain that's breaking my back, eating me up inside. I forget who and where I am. You think I'm exaggerating, that I'm telling you this to pretend I'm an intellectual. I didn't get very far in school. I would have liked to be a creative person like you, but I don't have it in me. Ever since you began telling us tales from the *Thousand and One Nights,* survival here has been more bearable than it was before. I would never have thought that I would love listening to stories so much. When we were in Ahermemou, I used to watch you, and I noticed that after every leave you came back with books. Me, I brought back decks of cards, and cakes my mother made. I envied you. You remember one day I asked you to lend me a book? You gave me some poems to read. I tried to understand, but I gave up. Another time, you gave me a detective story. I liked it a lot, but it was set in America. I would have liked something that took place in our own country, in my hometown, in Rachidia. I'm saying all this to tell you that you absolutely have to go back to taking us traveling with your stories. It's not just to pass the time anymore, now it's so we don't croak—yes, I have the feeling that if I stop hearing your stories, I'll waste away. I know you haven't got much strength left, that your voice is hoarse from the cold, that you've lost another tooth this week, but I'm begging you, come back to work!"

Touched by his request, I promised that after the evening starches I would tell him the story of the beautiful twin girls who marry two dwarf brothers. Unfortunately, I was knocked out by a high fever and fell asleep sitting in my corner, leaning my head against the cold wall. I could not speak or get up and was only semiconscious, hearing noises but understanding nothing of what went on around me. For several days, to my surprise, I lost my bearings. I had no idea where I was or what I was doing in that hole. I was delirious, my fever got worse, and then, one morning, after a week of absence, I woke up, exhausted. My head was spinning, and the first thing I said was Abdelkader's name. Lhoucine told me they had come for him the day before. They had put him in a plastic bag and dragged the body out the door. When they were gone, the Ustad recited from the Koran. Abdelkader had let himself die, he was a suicide, because he had vomited blood. He must have swallowed something sharp. I will never know. I tell myself he would have died even if I'd had the strength to tell him stories. He clung to the words, they were his last hope. He often assured me that he was my friend and he trusted that one day, he would get out of there to let that friendship blossom in the open air. He was the kind who shares everything, gives everything. He told me once, "With you, I'd share all that God gives me, all, including my shroud!" A guard told me later that he was buried without a shroud, without any ritual preparation, just thrown into the raw earth and covered with quicklime.

15

For the first time in my life, something powerful and unshakable had taken hold of me. I knew that my mother was never one to change her mind. When she banished my father from the house, throwing his belongings out into the street, he sent her messengers, bouquets of flowers, fine silks—but no matter what he tried, he got nowhere. She would have nothing more to do with him in her house or her life. This firmness was something she had inherited from her own mother, who was called Madame General, a shrewd woman of spirit who stood up to men, was affectionate with her children, and harbored no illusions about the world. My mother often held her up as an example.

I thought of these two women when I realized that I would survive, that I would not be defeated. This intuition was strong and unambiguous. In the beginning, during those first months and years, I'd had no sense of the future. I had been drained of both hope and the ability to sense what was coming. Abdelkader's death affected me greatly, perhaps because I felt I could have helped him, as he had asked me to do, and then maybe he would have hung on a few more months. I had known that he was sick, but when he breathed his last, I had been too ill even to be aware of his passing, and I felt miserable over it. I suppose he must have called to me for comfort in his final moments. Maybe he knew that I was unconscious and struggling with fever! I would have liked so much to have told him one more story, to have transported him on the wings of a superb bird that would have flown off with him toward paradise.

One certainty: whatever the degree of faith and belief of these companions killed by suffering and sadness, they deserved to go to paradise. They endured a vengeance of infinite cruelty. Even if they had made mistakes, even if they had done wrong, what they went through in that subterranean dungeon was the most fearsome barbarity.

From the moment I began to tell myself such things, I was utterly convinced that our executioners would not get the better of me. Sometimes I even felt different from the other prisoners. I was ashamed. I prayed for my soul and theirs. I entered silence and immobility. I breathed deeply and invoked the supreme light that dwelled in my mother's heart, in the hearts of men and women of goodwill, in the souls of the prophets, saints, and martyrs, in the minds of those who have resisted and triumphed over misfortune through the sole power of the spirit, the power of inner prayer, which has no goal, which takes you toward the center of gravity of your own conscience.

That light was the guiding strength of the mind. I was prepared to abandon my body to our tormentors, as long as they did not seize hold of my soul, my breath, my will. Sometimes I thought about Muslim mystics who went into seclusion and renounced everything through the boundless love of God. Certain holy men, accustomed to suffering, tame this suffering and make it their ally: it leads them so close to God that they become one with Him and lose their reason. Thus the deepest affliction cleaves their hearts wide open. At times it opened certain windows in the heavens for me. I had not reached that glorious stage at which the mystics offer up their bodies to the sobbing of light, then do everything possible to hasten the hour of the decisive encounter. Afterward, they lose themselves in the exile of the sands.

As for me, I wanted to remain conscious and to master the little that was left to me. I absolutely did not have the soul of a martyr. I had no desire to declare that my blood was "permissable" and might be shed with impunity. I stamped on the ground as if to remind the madness stalking me that I would not be an easy prey.

My rheumatism made any movement difficult, if not impossible. I would sit on the chilly cement in the least uncomfortable position I could manage. It took hours for me to attain a state of insensibility to pain. My skin seemed to melt away. I left, went off on voyages. My thoughts became clear, simple, direct. Without moving, I let them carry me away. I concentrated until I actually became my own thoughts. When I reached this point, everything was easier. That is how I found myself, at night, alone in the deserted square of the Kaaba, facing the black stone. I approached it slowly. I caressed it. I felt as though I had been transported several centuries into the past, and at the same time wafted into a radiant future. I spent the night at the Kaaba, until dawn, the moment of the first prayer. People were performing their ablutions, praying, and they looked right through me. I was transparent. Only my spirit was there. This freedom could be enjoyed only rarely. I could not abuse it. I had to go back to the pit, to my body and my suffering.

The wind blowing my spirit to the east had died away. Nothing moved anymore. Not one leaf was trembling. This was the sign of my return. The voyage was over. I would live in expectation of another departure, one ear cocked in the direction of the ventilation shaft. I had become quite sensitive to the movement of air, the air that allowed us to survive, that brought us news of the world as it passed through and left heavy with our silence, our lassitude, and the odors of men steeped in the fetid dampness of death chambers where the condemned could not even rest in peace.

16

For a long time I had forgotten that I had a father. I did not think about him; he was not among the images that visited me. One day, I saw him in a dream: this man well known for his elegance of dress, upright carriage, and proud demeanor appeared to me on Jamaa El Fna Square* in Marrakech in a patched and dirty gandoura,* unshaven, with a weary face, and infinite sadness in his eyes. Standing next to a snake charmer, he was performing as a storyteller but had almost no audience. People would come by, look at him, then go on their way, leaving him alone in the middle of the tale of Antar the Brave rescuing Abla the Beautiful, who had poisoned her master. He was pitiful: a ruined man, humiliated, mocked by fate. While I was there, listening to him, he looked at me.

"Ah!" he exclaimed. "You're the son of the great sheik, the *fqih*,* the friend of poets and the king. But what are you doing here? Aren't you dead? Your father has already buried you. I was at your funeral. Seeking forgiveness for having had an unworthy son, he summoned the family, the authorities, and even newspaper reporters, then he cursed you and buried you. There was even a coffin he'd filled with your belongings, your books, and all the photographs in which you appeared. He made a speech, and I was the one who read the Koran over your supposed remains. So you're not dead! Come here, closer to me, don't be afraid. I know, I haven't any water to wash with now, I've lost weight, I live on beans the café owner on the corner sometimes gives me. I try to tell stories, partly to pass the time, partly to earn a few dirhams so I can buy myself a lovely djellaba of wool and silk. I've already ordered it. I've figured it out: at ten dirhams a day, I could be wearing it within a hundred days. You'll see, when I've got it, I'll be a different person, I'll once again be the man of letters and friend of the powerful I was in another life."

*   *   *

This vision of my father, with our situations reversed, made me smile. To think that at the moment I was seeing him in rags, he must have been busy entertaining the king! Perhaps he was playing cards with him, providing commentary larded with puns and sly insinuations salacious enough to tickle the royal funny bone.

As far as my father was concerned, not only was I dead, I had never even existed. He saw no one who might remind him that one of his sons was in prison. My mother refused to see him again, and he lived in the palace, at the king's every beck and call. My brothers and sisters had been profoundly wounded by this. I found out later that he had helped most of his children by obtaining scholarships and government jobs for them on the condition that my name never be spoken in his presence. From time to time his face would visit me, the face of a witty man with a feudal cast of mind so ingrained that nothing disturbed his placid self-certainty. I always saw him in white, majestic, as if he had escaped from a different time, a different century. I was not angry with him. I have never been angry with him. I neither admired him, as some of my brothers did, nor hated him. I was not indifferent to him, of course, but I had removed him from my life, just as he had done with me in my dream. In fact, he is the one who left without really going away. He married another woman and led a double life. He would drop by now and then, picking a time when my mother was off at work. He would take a few nice djellabas and disappear. My mother drew her own conclusions from this and closed her door against him once and for all. She went to a judge and asked for a divorce. I was ten years old. To me, this man I had seen so little of did not belong to our family. Thanks to my mother, I had no feeling for him, either good or bad. She did not speak ill of him, saying simply that he had another family, that she did not wish him any harm, that she preferred to make the situation clear with a clean break. She must have suffered, but let nothing show in her behavior.

I would think about all this, in the silence of our dungeon.

What could he have done? Even if I did not plan any of what happened, I had not disobeyed orders. I had entered the palace without any hesitation, I had committed an offense against the king and the trust he placed in my father. I was supposed to carry out orders from my superiors, but I could have refused to go along with the others—and would probably have been cut down by a burst of machine-gun fire. I could have switched sides and defended the monarchy. It never occurred to me. Maybe I was paralyzed at the sight of that massacre. I was frozen, staring, stunned, dry-mouthed, with the sun hitting me full in the face. I saw only a flurry of images, and I just could not move. Ten years in prison was a heavy sentence, but a light one compared with what we were enduring in the prison of slow death. Could my father have left the court? No. When you serve the king, you do not resign your post. You submit, you obey, you always reply, "Yes, Your Majesty," you try to escape attention, you never ask the king to repeat himself, even if you have not clearly heard his order, you say, "N'am, Sidna," and do your best to figure out what he wanted. My father lived in that world, proudly and happily. Later I would hear about the son of an important personage with the title of "Special Representative of His Majesty." The son, a left-wing militant, had been condemned to fifteen years in prison for plotting against state security. It was a time of general paranoia. They were locking up students, often brilliant ones, simply for voicing the wrong opinions. It was also the period when General Oufkir,* minister of the interior, ordered that an administrative memorandum be read over the radio to announce the immediate Arabization of the teaching of philosophy, a move intended to weed out so-called subversive texts that had inspired student demonstrations. It seems the king summoned his special representative and upbraided him harshly for neglecting his son's education. This venerable man, of great moral and political integrity, had a stroke and remained in a coma for several years.

My father was not prepared to fall into a coma for anyone. It was not his way to feel responsible for his offspring. So what was the use of rehashing this question? He would have said, "I have no son," or "This man is not my son," but I have never said, and will never say, "I have no father," or "This man is not my father," even if I had more reasons than he to renounce our relationship.

I knew things were not that simple. I was doing whatever I could to stay alive. I remember that when we first landed in our dungeon, Rushdie, my friend from Fez, asked me, "Do you think your father, who's so important, could get us out of here?"

"Impossible," I replied. "He doesn't know what's happened. No one does. That's the whole point of this place. My family thinks we're in prison in Kenitra. No visits allowed. Besides, my father sees the king only to entertain him, not to discuss problems of state. So you see, it's better just to forget that I have a father, and especially that he has a position at court."

"When we were still normal prisoners," Rushdie told me, "my father went to see an officer he knew from their lycée days together. The man told him he had to appeal to someone higher up—a polite way of refusing to help. But, after all, you're right, no one can do anything for us. We've got to deal with this all by ourselves. Which means die all by ourselves. We don't exist anymore. We're dead men, and I'm sure we've been crossed off every government register. So what's the good of cramming our heads with crazy hopes? I just talk—I talk a lot because it makes me feel that I exist and even that I'm fighting back. But we've been utterly forgotten. We're oblivion itself. Sometimes I seriously think that I'm dead, that we're in the great beyond, in hell. I believe it so deeply that it makes me cry. I tell this to you and the others who understand me: sometimes I break down and sob like a kid. Can you imagine? A guy from a wealthy family, toughened by the army, and he's got tears pouring down his cheeks. I don't see anything shameful in that, but it's the only proof I've got that I'm not dead. You've read a great deal, you tell me: do you think that after this hole, when we return to life and die of indigestion or in a car crash—do you think we'll go to paradise?"

"Only God knows. I can't answer that question. But do what I do, pray, and don't think about any reward. You have to pray without expecting anything in return. That's the strength of faith."

"I don't understand what you mean, Salim."

"I pray to the infinite. I pray to God so that I can withdraw from the world. But the world comes down to so very, very little, as you know. I'm struggling not against the world, but against the feelings that prowl around us, trying to pull us toward the well of hatred. I don't pray *for,* but *with.* I don't pray in hopes of something, but against the weariness of survival. I pray against the lassitude that threatens to strangle us. So, my dear Rushdie, prayer is completely gratuitous."

Several images would go through my head. They would merge into one another, stumble, fall to the ground, or set off toward a gray horizon. Black-and-white images. My head refused to accept color. I would see my father walking, often bowing down, bending over as if to pick up something valuable. Ahead of him, the king. Striding confidently. Now and then turning around to make a mollifying gesture with his hand. My father would hurry along yet remain more than a yard behind the king. Observing proper etiquette, most likely. My father's mind was allowed no rest. He had to invent witticisms, puns, jokes that were salacious but never vulgar. And it was most important that he launch his sallies at just the right moment. To be a court jester, a magician, a shrewd psychologist, a mind reader, a clairvoyant, a comforting presence: that was my father's function.

He had to anticipate, forestall, react quickly. It was more than a profession or a vocation.

The mind constantly on alert. No fatigue, no relaxation, no doubts. No relief for his brain and memory. Which didn't leave him one minute to think about his son. Did he know to what hell his patron had exiled me? And even if he had known, what would he have said or done? Nothing.

It was vital that I get rid of these images. When I swept them away with the back of my hand, they would flood back in, coming ever nearer, in still more detail. I had never seen my father's face at such close range. It was striking. His skin was scarred from a childhood illness, so he covered the marks with foundation makeup. Like a woman, like a coquette, my father took meticulous care of his face. The other image, that of the king, was fixed and inscrutable. He was always peering off into the distance. Perhaps there was a thought behind that mysterious gaze, a thought about us? What I mean is, I dared to suppose that he was thinking of us. Sometimes I even wondered, does he know? Is he aware that we exist underground? A man shaken by two coups d'état cannot forget about the rebels, naturally. Wait . . . I said "rebels"? Me, I was no more of a rebel than any other Moroccan citizen disgusted by the widespread corruption and indignation forced upon an entire people. But I was a soldier with a weapon, a junior officer who obeyed orders. Why had they dragged us from the prison in Kenitra to throw us into this hole? What kind of logic was that? Ah, the tiny drop of water on the shaven skull! Ah, Chinese torture, Moroccan-style, with a brutality that slowly sinks into oblivion! Ah, redemption through lingering and pernicious suffering! There was no logic, just a relentless punishment that stretched out through time and engulfed the entire body.

I was brooding over those words in that strange dream when the image of the king approached and spoke to me.

"Stand at attention! I know, you can't stand up. You bang your head on the ceiling. So stay crouched there and listen to

me carefully. Stop wondering if I ever think about you. I have
better things to do than think about a pack of criminals and
traitors. You raised your hand against your king—I know that
you did not use your weapon—and you must regret that for the
rest of your life, simply learn to regret it, in this hole, until the
Last Judgment. Your father neglected to raise you properly, not
I, and that's just how it is. So don't bring my image into this
stinking dungeon anymore. I forbid you to think of me or to
mix my image in with others!"

I was dumbfounded. Was that really his voice? I admit that I
had forgotten what it sounded like. But a king does not deign to
speak to a poor junior officer who cannot even stand up.

17

Number 6, Majid, kept asking Karim what time it was. You would have thought he had an appointment or that he was waiting for a train. He would repeat the time after Karim, then carry on a rambling conversation.

"That's good, that's excellent, we're getting close to our objective. Mind you, that depends not just on what time it is, but on the day as well. Karim, tell me, please, what day is it?"

"Today is Saturday."

"Then excuse me, I've got the wrong day. In theory, if he comes, it will be on a Friday, right after the midday prayer."

"But who are you talking about?"

"What, you don't know, you who can tell time with diabolical precision?"

"Well, that's it, keeping track of the time doesn't allow me to pay attention to anything else."

"Moha. You know, the man who always tells the truth, because he has nothing to lose. He'll come set us free. It's not a joke. I haven't gone nuts. I'm in contact with him through my thoughts. We talk to each other. He often tells me to have patience. I reply that patience can't be bought in the marketplace anymore. That makes him laugh. Ah, patience! It's true—that's all we have left. Me, I've acquired enough of it to share some with whoever wants to go with me. When Moha comes, he'll be invisible, but he'll announce his arrival with the perfume of paradise. Keep your nostrils wide open. Mustn't miss this chance!"

No one argued with Majid. A Berber from Agadir, he was short, lean, with a twinkle in his sharp eyes. It was the cigarettes that drove him out of his mind. He smoked two packs a day. At the Military Academy he sometimes woke in the middle of the night to smoke. Every winter he coughed his lungs out. Cigarettes were his drug, his reason for being, his passion, his purpose in life. He did not like army-issue tobacco. All his money was spent on cartons of American cigarettes.

After almost ten years of prison, he still could not forget tobacco. His cough had gotten worse. Perhaps nicotine would have soothed it. With time he had stopped begging for cigarettes, but now he wandered from one subject to another. He had invented Moha, this providential person who kept him company. Moha could travel through space and time and make himself invisible. Majid claimed to hear him. At first I thought that he was striving for spiritual enlightenment, that like myself he was escaping his body—in his case, to avoid the suffering of nicotine craving. That might have been one outlet for his pain. I quickly realized my mistake, however. Poor Majid was not one of us anymore. He had lost his wits. He no longer talked about Moha but about all the companions we had buried.

"Those you've laid to rest are not dead. I know it. I'm the only one who does. So I'm telling you this: they're pretending. Be ready to join them. They're waiting for us on the other side of the hill. They're all there: Larbi, Abdelkader, Mustapha, Driss, Rushdie, Hamid . . . They're playing dead to fool the guards. They're waiting for the right moment to make their getaway. The quicklime poured on their bodies warms and wakes them up. Not only do they run off, but while they're at it, they throw the guards into their graves. That's why some of the guards limp. Soon we'll have the great escape, freedom at last, and we'll smoke all the cigarettes in the world."

His friend Karim tried to reason with him. Majid would pretend to listen and even to agree with him, then go off into his rigmarole, insisting more and more that the dead men were not dead but were out there preparing our escape. He had his own peculiar logic.

"Karim, listen, you know perfectly well there's only one way out of here: feet first. So everyone who has left us realized that they had to play dead, get themselves swiftly buried, then jump out of the quicklime and go hide in the woods nearby, to come back well armed and rescue us. I swear to you it's true. I'm not making this up. It's even said in the Koran, and Ustad Gharbi can confirm this, that those who die unjustly are alive with God."

Gharbi intervened to set the record straight.

"You're talking about martyrs. I don't know if we fit God's definition of martyrs."

With that, we struck up a discussion that was half religious, half political. Who were we? What was our status? Were we disloyal soldiers? Political prisoners? Victims of injustice? We had been sent here after serving one-fifth of our sentence. We had been kidnapped from Kenitra and thrown into this pit. Justice, their justice, the one that had paraded before the press, before our stunned eyes, as we stood there in clean shirts with our heads shaved, had tricked us. We were soldiers led astray by our superior officers. They had armed us and told us, a few minutes before we arrived at Skhirate, "Our king is in danger, let's save him. Our enemies are disguised as guests and golfers!" Who were we at that moment: deceived cadets or consenting traitors? How can you know what goes on in the head of a junior officer when he finds himself dazzled by such a blinding light, on his own, machine gun in hand, and he hears the order to fire?

At one point, the putting green of the golf course had caught my eye: it was so beautifully cut, so even, so bright, so *green,* a subtle, perfectly flawless green. I was walking on that lawn, as comfortable underfoot as a handsome carpet, when a man—a foreigner, I think—called out to me.

"No, no, not in your combat boots! You're ruining this green! No, go walk somewhere else, or take off your boots."

Meanwhile, bullets were whistling in every direction and

well-dressed men with impeccably combed hair were dropping like flies. I left the golf course without truly realizing the seriousness of what was happening. I even forgot the apprehensions and suspicions I had silently shared with Rushdie.

Ever since that precise moment, I have been unable to make sense of that tragedy. Killing the king! But what would have been the use of that? To replace him with a military junta? Generals, lieutenant colonels who would have shared power and divided up the country's assets? I have thought a great deal about this and have come to believe that it was lucky we failed. No, what I mean is—luckily, they failed! Oh, what a military dictatorship Commandant A. and his adjutant, Atta, would have cooked up for us! I knew them well. I am in a prime position to understand and speak about this. But who can still hear me, in this hole?

Majid spoke to me as if he had read my mind.

"You're right. Moha agrees with you. What can you expect from soldiers who believe in force more than in justice? If we wound up here, in this tunnel, it's their fault. They didn't ask for our opinion. Anyway, in the army you don't try to find out what cadets are thinking. That's why we have to escape. There's only the dead men's ruse to help us. The living can't do a thing for us. But we're dead, too. We're trapped in hell, it's a mistake, an unfortunate judicial error. The proof that we're pretending to be alive is that the very ones we think are dead are only pretending to be dead and are waiting for us to leave the country with them."

I decided not to argue with him. Why bother? He was surviving on that hope. He said he was waiting for Moha. When Karim tired of his constant requests for the time and told him that the clock was broken, Majid wept. I had to do something, reassure him in some way, outsmart his madness. I made believe I was Moha and talked to him. I had no trouble speaking for this person conjured up by Majid in his despair. I was Moha. I had his presence, his voice, and his confidence.

"O Impatient One, whose time keeps burning up, swallowed by this motionless night, you who believe that the dead are actors playing on a stage peopled by shadows and phantoms, you whose uneasiness grows in the darkness, know that I am only a distant murmur, a flame disguised as brightness, a word that rises from your entrails and then plummets into a well. The wind is heavy with sand and erases all footsteps, yet it carries my voice. You alone can lead yourself out of this tunnel. For this you will need a ferocious will, a strength of mind more powerful than dreams, more luminous than prayer. I do not live in lofty trees. I dwell in thoughts that hurt, that tear my skin yet bear me over sleeping forests and mountains. I am going away. I am already far off. I return you to yourself, to your solitude, and to your right mind!"

After these words came a long silence, broken by Karim's announcement of the time. Majid said nothing. A few days later, I sensed that he was agitated in his cell. I called to him; he did not reply. After the evening meal, we heard the sound of a struggling body.

Majid was the only one who managed to hang himself in that prison. He had tied his clothes together to make a rope, wrapped it around his neck, tightened it with all his strength, attached the end of his shirt to the ventilation grille, and lain down on the floor, pushing his feet against the door until he throttled himself.

He was completely naked. His body was battered. It looked as if cigarettes had been stubbed out on his skin. He weighed very little, and his bloodshot eyes were open.

His death was not a scene from a play. He wore no mask on his face. Alas! He was not pretending.

18

Fallen from the sky, like a message or a mistake. A pigeon—a dove?—had slipped into the central air shaft and landed in the silence of our dense darkness. Ustad Gharbi was categorical.

"It's a dove. I know what I'm talking about."

No one contradicted him. To us it was a phenomenon from heaven. Something besides a burial or an attack of illness. And it had come to us completely out of the blue.

The dove flew around bumping into walls. The Ustad called her by imitating the cooing of pigeons. She went toward his cell but found no opening to pass through. So she huddled in a corner and probably fell asleep. When the guards opened the first cell, she rushed in, becoming the guest of Mohammed. The guards never noticed a thing. As usual, they were in a hurry to distribute our rations and leave.

Mohammed was as happy as a kid. He talked to the dove, told us it was a sign from fate, that we had to take care of her and make her a messenger.

"We'll adopt her, give her a name. She'll be our companion, and we'll train her to take messages to the outside world, to our families, maybe even to the human rights activists . . ."

"You should pass her to me," retorted the Ustad. "I'll teach her to say the name of God. All doves know Allah."

Bourras, Number 13, a quiet man by nature, became quite excited about this visitor.

"We'll call her Hourria: Freedom!"

"Hourria!" said Mohammed, feeding the dove. "O our Freedom, you came here to bring us a message. I'm sure you didn't land here by chance. Who could have sent you? There's no ring or letter in your claws. So it was God who directed you to this hole."

His neighbor, Fellah, Number 14, was positively lyrical.

"O my dove, symbol of peace and joy, if you are here today, it's because God has taken pity on us, and a royal pardon has been issued in our favor. After all, we're not responsible for what other men did."

Our talking clock spoke up without hesitation.

"It would not be within palace protocol to alert us by sending a dove. If they do pardon us one day, the tip-off will be when they give us better food and send a doctor to examine us. If we're to be released, we'll have to be in good health. That said, this dove is a blessing from God. It's a little diversion for us."

Mohammed disagreed.

"A diversion? No, an event. Someone is contacting us. For the moment, the dove will stay with me. She'll keep me company."

The others protested.

"No, she belongs to all of us," said Bourras.

"Let's be democratic," suggested Fellah. "We'll share her equally. She'll spend one day and night with each of us."

And that is how Hourria went from cell to cell while the guards were bringing us our meals. They laughed at us.

"Don't eat the dove alive, you'll get stomach cramps," said one.

"Maybe the bird's booby-trapped," added another. "It must carry a contagious disease. You should change its name and call it El Mout (Death)!"

For a few seconds, I believed him. But the perverse logic tormenting us did not square with that last hypothesis. I thought back to the episode of the scorpions and wondered once again if they had been introduced by the guards to poison us. The dove had arrived all by herself. She was an accidental dove. She preoccupied us for a good month or so. She slept with us, ate our starchy food. She shared our fate and showed no agitation or desire to leave. One day, however, we decided to set her free. It was Mohammed who first mentioned this.

"There's no reason to keep this creature a prisoner here. It would be better to let the bird go."

"But we'll miss her!" said Bourras.

"That's true," chimed in Karim. "We've gotten used to having her around."

I would really have liked to attach a message to her leg, a cry for help, just so people would know that we were not all dead. But I had no paper, pencil, or string. So I spoke to her as if in a dream.

"Hourria, when you have regained your freedom, when you're out in the light and you fly up toward the sky, stop a moment on the terrace of a house, my house, the one where I was born, where my mother lives. She's in Marrakech, in the medina. You'll recognize the terrace: it's the only one painted blue, whereas all the others are red. The door is always open. You land and you go into the courtyard. In the center, a lemon tree and a well. My mother likes to rest there. You go to her and alight on her shoulder. I'm sure she'll understand that I've sent you. Simply look at her and she will read my message in your eyes: dear Mama, I'm alive, I love you, don't worry about me. Thanks to God, thanks to faith, I'll pull through. I think of you often. I'm furious with myself for hurting you by having acted as I did. Take care of yourself, it's important. Tell my little brother that I think about him a lot, tell Mahi I've learned to play cards and when I get out I'll show him I'm a champion. Tell my sisters they are in my thoughts. I'll see you very soon. May God keep you for us all, a diadem above our heads, shedding grace and light upon us."

Everyone wanted to do the same thing, to load her with messages, so that she would bear witness to our distress. I held her gently on my lap as their words streamed from the cells.

"My father lives in El Hajeb. Tell him his Abdeslam is alive!"

"Tell my fiancée, Zoubida, to wait for me. I'll be out soon!"

"Go to the tomb of my parents in Taza and say a prayer . . ."

"Go to Skhirate and crap on the golf course."

"Tell my sister Fatima to marry our cousin. I can't come to their wedding . . ."

"Let Amnesty International know about the conditions we live in!"

"Go, fly free . . . Enjoy your liberty!"

"Don't forget to go to the mosque and ask them to say the prayer for the absent one several times, for all of us who have died . . ."

"If you go to Jamaa El Fna, in Marrakech, stop at the house of the pigeon master, the one who trains them to put on plays. As soon as he sees you, he'll know where you've come from and what message you bring."

"Me, I'm not asking you for anything. I've got no message to send, or rather, I've got nobody to send one to. So go wherever you want, come back when you like, and tell the other pigeons we're expecting them."

The dungeon was like the souk* on auction day. Everybody was talking to that poor dove as if she were capable of delivering each message. I could hardly reproach my companions when I had been the one who started it all. Now a current of madness was flowing through the prison. Frenzy, cacophony, incomprehensible words, absurd images. The dove was no longer a bird but a person come to harvest messages from every side.

The next morning, as soon as the door opened, I set her free. She whirled around in fright until a guard caught her and shooed her toward the exit.

We missed her. We thought of her with a smile, realizing how truly miserable we were.

19

Dying of constipation. No one had thought of that. People say "dying of love" or "dying of hunger and thirst." Bourras died because he could not expel his excrement. He was holding it in, or rather, an inner force was keeping it from coming out, it was piling up day after day and growing as hard as concrete. Poor Bourras did not dare talk about it. He stopped eating, hoping to get rid of everything that had built up inside him. Unable to bear it anymore, he moaned and kicked at the walls, and then one day he let out a cry so piercing and prolonged that the guards had to investigate. They did nothing, just sized up the situation and burst out laughing. The more they laughed, the more Bourras wailed.

"I'm going to die smothered in shit! I can't wait any longer, give me some medicine, I'm begging you, something to dissolve this block of cement . . ."

No reply. They slammed the door shut. You could hear them chuckling and making fun of him.

"Disturbing us because he can't crap!"

"And then he wants us to help him! Can you just see yourself digging for shit up his ass with a little spoon? Yuck!"

"Stop, you're going to make me throw up . . ."

"If it kills him, can you picture the Kmandar writing a report to headquarters to say Number 13 died because he couldn't crap?"

"What a load of shit!"

"You said it—a load of shit!"

Lhoucine carved a sort of spoon out of the broomstick he had kept.

"Here, I'm tossing you this piece of wood. Try gently, don't force anything or hurt yourself, and, above all, calm down."

In the indecent quiet, we all waited to see how things would go, imagining this swollen man. When you think that a suppository or a little castor oil would have been enough to relieve him . . . But we were not in life. We were in a death pit. Each to his own bad luck. Who would have thought that this strapping man, a burly guy from the mountains, would one day die with his belly distended like a balloon?

I could hear him, envision him, and I was afraid. It might happen to any one of us. We got no exercise, always ate the same tasteless, starchy food without any spices. I resolved to do gymnastics more regularly in the future, insofar as it was possible. I was cramped for space, but even crouching or sitting down, I tried to move my arms and legs, to hop, to do simple, useful exercises. I would lie on my back, feet against the wall, then draw my knees up close to my chest. Then I would duck-walk back and forth. My muscles had to get a workout.

Bourras pushed too hard with the piece of wood and perforated his rectum. There was no bowel movement, only blood. At some point, he had another fit of frustration, howled one last great cry, and collapsed. Exhausted by so much effort, he must have passed out. He died the following day. Death relaxed his sphincter, and his body voided everything. The stink of blood and shit made us gag. The guards were not laughing anymore when they found him.

"We could have saved him," they told us in some embarrassment, holding their hands over their mouths and noses. "We thought he was trying to fool us. Bourras was always playing tricks, you know that . . . Who would've believed constipation could kill you? Well, all this will have to be cleaned up, unless the Kmandar decides that you deserve this shit."

Was it from selfish motives or pity? We learned from another guard that, from then on, some kind of laxative was mixed in with our meals. There were no more tragic cases of constipation.

The grotesque aspects of certain situations kept us from feeling despondent. Basically, we did not have much use for sadness. We were not happy or sad. Sorrow rolled right off us. As soon as one of us let himself fall into the trap of melancholy, he wasted away. A depressed person is lucky: he is living a normal life—because his depression is a passing moment in his life, not a permanent state. Even with the cruelest misfortune, there comes a time when forgetting begins, and discouragement fades. But we did not have that option. Because with us, sadness was a slight irritation, a minor injury to be treated with a dab of alcohol. Down in our hole we had no right to weep. There was no one to dry our tears. Those who cried knew they were not long for this world. Tears flowed to wash the face soon to be kissed by death.

That night, I became disoriented. Was I awake or was it an absurd dream where everything was jumbled together? Death in a white robe, with butterflies—live butterflies—glued on? Something was wrong there . . . Other images flitted through my aching head.

The millstone. The house. Head downward. I'm walking on my hands. I'm rotting. In a hole, I should add. The head has fallen off. The ground is tilting. The millstone is turning. It's my head I see, tossed into the middle of the courtyard. Next to the dead trunk of an old olive tree. I run into the house. My mother is calling me. My voice is locked up in my throat. It's a holiday. I am absent. I see all of them. No one sees me. I'm floating on brackish water. I search for the source. I search for the sea. Look, a spider. It eclipses the sun. I reach out to touch the light, to fall into its blinding brightness. I'm not tired. My mother is burning incense. My sisters climb up on the table and dance. Someone says, "I've been caught short." I bite my right hand. I lose three teeth all at once. I tug on my thick mop of hair. Not one strand pulls out. Ants live in my beard. No, not lice. I said ants. They come and go. I shake my beard. They hold on tight. Death walks by. Seems in a hurry. The black stone is on one scale of the balance. On the other, I place a ring. The millstone rolls forward and topples everything over.

20

There was a period when I stopped frequently on the path of spirituality to meditate, learning simple but essential things.

In the exercise I was perfecting to achieve greater concentration, I would see a woman in the night. She always had her back to me, and when she spoke, I listened without trying to see her face. Moving slowly forward, she would ask me to follow her in her pilgrimage around the seven saints of Marrakech, the guardian spirits of survivors, the poor, and the dead.

Seven men. Seven stations. Seven prayers. Faces turned to eternity, a lesson in renunciation, an apprenticeship in solitude and the elevation of the soul. I was familiar with the seven saints. When I was little, my mother would take me with her to visit them, one by one. She would speak to them as though they could hear her, as though they were alive in their tombs covered with green or black silk embroidered with Koranic calligraphy in gold thread. She told them about her life, her trials and sorrows. She asked them for help, for the strength to carry on. And I would listen to my mother, not wanting to disturb her. She was not the only one making these rounds. So many women, so many unhappy wives, weeping mothers, unmarried girls, and women unable to have children! The husband of a neighbor of ours had disappeared. Two men had come for him to show him a house for sale—he was a real estate agent—and he had never returned. His children had gone to the police, who always said the same thing: "We're continuing our inquiries. As soon as we have a lead, we'll get in touch with you." But everyone knew that the man had been kidnapped and dumped in a ditch. It seems his crime was to have been mixed up in some shady business about a villa confiscated by a powerful police official from a foreigner expelled from Morocco on a morals charge. Instructed by the owner to sell the villa, the real estate agent had been advised that he should forget about the property; it was not for sale and no longer belonged to the Frenchman. He did not take this advice seriously, and so he disappeared.

His wife, our neighbor, set out every Friday to speak to the seven saints.

"Let me have justice! Let my man come back to me! If he's dead, if they've killed him, let me be told. I don't sleep anymore. I've prepared his shroud and I'm waiting. I've also prepared the wedding chamber. When he returns, we'll get married again, as we did the first day we met. We won't make a child, but we'll make endless love. Intercede for me with the Prophet, with the Source of Truth, with the light that shines from your tomb, to tell me where my husband is! Here, no one listens to me, no one answers me. Here, men are cowards . . ." She had hung a padlock on the bars of one of the mausoleum windows, closed the lock, and thrown the key into the gutter. She returned every Thursday to see if the padlock had been opened, a sign that fate would send her husband back to her.

In my night, I followed that shadow. She was not my mother. Maybe my mother had sent her to me. Was my mother unwell? That must have been the message. I had to concentrate even harder to confirm this intuition. My mother and that woman looking for her vanished husband, my mother and that shadow whose steps I followed—they spoke to me in my profound silence. I felt quite sure. I no longer had any doubt: my mother was ill. With this idea, I fell back into my aching body. I had seen her pale face, her feverish eyes. She was in pain. It was not a passing sickness. No, my mother was in grave danger. That was the image I would live with, and it gave me even more courage and strength to resist.

*   *   *

At this stage on the path of spirituality, I had quite naturally entered "the house of limpid solitude," where lamentation was useless, but where each stone, each moment of silence, was a mirror that reflected the soul—now light and confident, now bruised and grave. This house was my victory, my absolute secret, a mysterious garden to which I escaped. I left my cell on tiptoe. Abandoning the carcass of my body, I would fly off to the sunny terraces of that spacious villa. Although somewhat dilapidated, it welcomed me and offered the advantage, at the end of my night, of restoring my desire to keep going.

There, I was at leisure to think about the black stone and the pilgrimage I promised myself I would make. Why choose the Kaaba, Mecca, and Medina? Those sacred places belonged to the religion in which I was raised. I felt that religion should remain a personal thing. But how many times had I been told that Islam was our community, our identity, that we formed a nation, the best and most beautiful created by God? I had renounced prayer when I was in Ahermemou. I believed in God, but sometimes I had my doubts. Since being condemned to the slow death of bodily decay, I had called unceasingly upon God. The nearness of death, the destruction of all dignity, the perverse oppression lurking around me had pushed me onto the path of this transparent solitude.

My garden is humble. A few orange trees, one or two lemon trees, a well of cool water in the center, lush grass, and a room in which to sleep when it's cold or rainy. In this room there is nothing, just a mat, a pillow, and a blanket. The walls have been limewashed in blue. When the daylight fades, I light two candles and read. In the evening, I eat vegetables from the garden. An old peasant woman who lives in the area brings me bread every day at the same hour. That is my secret, my dream life, the place where I like to go to meditate. To pray and think about those who are no longer here. I do not need anything else. Above all, one must possess nothing, acquire nothing, be light, in good spirits, ready to walk off and leave everything behind, wearing only a simple djellaba to cover the body. There is nothing like complete renunciation to take your mind off death. But although mine no longer preoccupied me, I was still moved by the death of my companions. We all should have reached this state of renunciation and triumphed together over death. But disease, slow deterioration, suffering—that was the real face of death. A yawning chasm. Some walked in the darkness without leaving their cells, then fell through the trapdoor that shunted them into the damp earth.

When I was in the garden, I was happy. I felt unfettered by time, memory, injustice, and all the evil that had been done to us. But I could not get into my garden simply because I felt like going. I had to take the time to work myself free of my shell, to enter another world. It was not easy. Successful concentration demanded special conditions—silence was not enough. I never achieved complete fulfillment because I could not always forget my pain, especially during the period when I was losing my teeth. Not only were the toothaches excruciating but they made me fall back and lose the thread of my voyage toward an ideal spirituality. It would be impossible to reflect, to think, to resist. That was a torture we all experienced. More than once I tried to tear out a molar and wound up with it half hanging on a strip of living flesh, doubling my agony. I had managed to master my body during the dreadful cold, the stifling heat, and my bouts of rheumatism, but I was defeated by my toothaches.

Our bodies were rotting limb by limb. The only thing I possessed was my mind, my reason. I abandoned my arms and legs to our tormentors, hoping they would not manage to claim my spirit, my freedom, my breath of fresh air, my gleam of light in the darkness. Ignoring their strategy, I threw up barricades around myself. I learned to renounce my body. The body is what is visible. They saw it, they could touch it, cut it with a red-hot blade, they could torture it, starve it, expose it to scorpions, to biting cold, but I strove to keep my mind out of reach. That was my sole strength. I opposed the brutality of our captors with my seclusion, my indifference, my insensibility. Actually, I was neither indifferent nor insensible, but I was training myself to withstand what they were doing to us. How could you be indifferent? You hurt, your skin is pierced by rusty metal, blood flows, your tears as well, you think of something else, you try with all your might to escape, to conjure up some greater suffering. You will not get out of there by imagining a field of red poppies or white daisies. No, that escape is brief, not mysterious enough. It's even too easy. At first I would go off into meadows, but suffering would quickly haul me back into the hole. That is when I understood that you had to erase one pain by imagining an even more horrendous one.

Luckily, my imagination was unharmed. It fed on anything. I could spin a whole story out of a chance word from one of my companions. I loved to guess the history of words. "Coffee," for example. I spent hours fantasizing about where the beans come from, who discovered them, how somebody thought of roasting them just enough so that they could then be ground, and how someone tried boiling this dark brown powder, filtering the resulting liquid, drinking it with or without sugar, adding a touch of cinnamon or other spices, and how coffee became known throughout the world, a drug for some, a stimulant for others, a habit for everyone. I pictured fields of bushes producing green coffee beans on sunny mountainsides. I calculated the time required between the day when the shrub is planted and the morning when I could enter a café and ask— without even thinking about it, oblivious to my surroundings— for "Coffee, please, black and strong . . ." I imagined the journey, the stages, the intermediaries, the chain of vendors and buyers, the factories where they process several grades of coffee, I imagined how they mix arabica with robusta, how they select the finest harvests and reserve them for powerful people who demand the very best for their morning coffee. I thought of a palace where a king or prince will not get out of bed until he has had two cups of a good brisk arabica imported from Costa Rica, roasted by Italians, and prepared by a Neapolitan chef . . . I thought as well about how people can get nervous when they haven't had their coffee—or when they've had too much of it. I stopped getting the jitters a long time ago. It seems they put a bromide or some other sedative into our morning drink here so that our genitals don't act up. A cook had already told me that in Ahermemou. Once a week they poured some white powder into the big coffeepot, but never on the day before we went on leave. I knew this. The army sticks its nose everywhere. Nothing was supposed to escape its notice. Even when you were on the outside, with your family or in some whorehouse, the army was watching. You belonged to it in peacetime as in wartime. Where we were now, our bodies were meant to fall apart piece by piece. In my case, my penis was the first thing to go. I had forgotten all about it and had no trouble ignoring its existence and condition from then on. Which led me to reflect at length on sexuality in general and ours—in Morocco—in particular. I was not a psychologist or a sexologist, but I noticed certain behaviors in my companions when we were cadets at the Military Academy. I was like them: my sexuality was poor, impatient, and almost bestial. I remember our short leaves, the evening passes. In his kindness the commandant would select a dozen cadets to go empty their testicles in the nearest village. This was—unofficially—a "fuck pass." Everyone got his turn. I remember a house lighted by candles with an interior courtyard covered in carpets and surrounded by rooms piled high with other rugs. I remember a rather fat woman, sitting in the middle of one of these rooms, surrounded by four or five very young girls. An old woman emerged from the shadows, carrying a tea tray, followed by a little girl barely ten years old with a dish of honey crêpes. Everything happened in silence. My companions were more used to going there than I was. The fat woman, the owner of the place, called to one of us by name.

"We haven't seen you for a long time! You were being punished. The army has no pity for you, bulls shut up in their stalls! What a shame! When I think of my girls, who spend the day weaving carpets and asking me over and over if we'll have any visits this evening . . . I don't know what to say to them anymore."

We mumbled something or other. We drank tea and ate crêpes, looking the girls over, choosing our partners, or rather, our victims, because we performed quickly and badly. We were in a hurry to get it over with, to pay these unfortunate mountain girls and start thinking about the next time. After tea, the owner would blow out the candles, and each of us would go off with a girl, without a word, as if everything had been arranged beforehand. In the darkness we could hear whispers, panting, and after a few minutes, a muffled cry, the cry of a man shooting his load. When we stood up again, the girls would stay lying on their backs, their legs spread. Some of them said, *"Hadou houma rejal! Bhal lbrak!"* ("Just like a man! In and out!") We would stand around a little sheepishly, anxious to leave. Then we lined up and pissed against the wall across the street, convinced that we were getting rid of any germs we might have caught. I never felt proud of myself. Each time I resolved never to return to the house of fat Kaouada, the rug merchant and madam.

21

That kind of memory was unimportant to me. I did not bother removing and burning it, as I had with the others. It was not even a memory. It was a series of gray images from a time when we were somewhat carefree, limiting our ambitions to being good soldiers, future officers in the Royal Armed Forces. Our studies were not at an advanced level, but we did not turn out too badly. I loved to read. It was my passion. After each home leave, I came back with books I had bought in Fez. The bookseller was a rather old man, quite nearsighted. He told me he sold books because he loved women, who were his chief clients. He was familiar with their tastes, their preferences. Like a doctor or a perfumer, he knew what to advise this or that female reader. He had thousands of volumes piled up in a disorder only he could understand. For me, he set aside classic French novels and Arab poetry. Reading was the invisible door I plunged through to escape that military school, to forget the violence of the training, and above all to block out the illiterate noncoms shouting their orders in a garbled language midway between French and Arabic: "felleen" for "fall in," "gzem" for "exempt," "birmissiou" for "permission," and so on.

When I was in the hole, entire pages of *Père Goriot* would come back to me in my solitude, often at incongruous moments, for example when I had a toothache and could no longer open my mouth. The words and sentences would stream by, and I would hear myself saying them as if I were reading to a sick child or in a classroom giving a dictation exercise. It was like a blessing from God. Through His grace, my memory recovered hundreds of pages read years earlier. I could recall them effortlessly: they scrolled past me all by themselves.

"Toward the end of the third year, old Goriot reduced his expenses still further by moving up to the fourth floor and budgeting himself at forty-five francs for his monthly room and board. He gave up tobacco, dismissed his hairdresser, and stopped using powder."

Some of my companions laughed at this passage, observing that a man should not wear powder. How could I explain to them the social and political context of the times in which Balzac wrote? I simply shrugged and continued.

"Goriot was an elderly libertine, and only a doctor's skill had saved his eyes from the evil side effects of the medications prescribed for his ailments."

"What's an elderly libertine?"

Off I would go into an analysis of the words and text, which led us far from the novel and often ended in a political discussion about our society, its customs, its hypocrisies and lies. And when I recited the tender letters Rastignac received from his mother and sisters, my audience made fun of them in disbelief.

"Tell us a story from a western, or a police thriller. We need real action!"

I continued my "reading," even if that bored some of my listeners. I did it to exercise my memory and keep from becoming confused.

When I was extremely tired, pages of Balzac and Victor Hugo would sometimes bombard me all mixed up together. The mess in my head gave me migraines, as if the elements of this clutter were so incompatible that I just could not bear it. "You've got to calm down," I'd tell myself. "You're lucky to have a good—a very good—memory. Relax, and everything will fall back into place!"

That notorious memory . . . It was all our father gave us. Like most of my brothers and sisters, I'm gifted in that department. My little brother, the one who went to the United States and studied at the Actors Studio, can recite every poem in *The Flowers of Evil* without a single hesitation or mistake.

Losing that inner strength immediately affected my situation in the hole: my cell shrank. The walls closed in on me; the ceiling dropped. I had to react quickly and recover that ability to be in touch with distant and imaginary worlds.

"I cleaned out my memory," I reassured myself. "I threw away whatever was too painful to remember. I burned some things; maybe I didn't manage to get rid of it all, or else I made a mistake—I must have burned some books instead of the images and places of my adolescence. Well, I have to straighten everything out. I'm calming down. I'm inhaling slowly, from the abdomen, and exhaling slowly, I'm extending my right leg, rotating it in small circles. I lower my right leg and do the same thing with the left one. I reach out with both arms. I touch the walls. Sitting, I lift them up. I'm two inches from the ceiling. The walls must move back. I push them with the palms of my hands. I stand up, still hunched over, and try to raise the ceiling as though it were a lid. I will repeat this operation all day long. When I collapse in exhaustion, I will know that I have managed to gain an inch or so. The abstract problem—of memory—can be solved by acting on something concrete, the area of my incarceration. If I succeed in organizing my mental library, I am saved. The walls will no longer oppress me. If I escape in my mind by recovering the characters imagined by my novelists, I won't have a problem with my space anymore."

That was when I had a revelation.

"If your memory deserts you, invent your own characters!"

Actually, it was not a desertion. It was fatigue, weariness. I had read and reread *Père Goriot* so many times, followed by *Les Misérables,* that the recording mechanism had jammed. New pages were needed, stories I had read only once. I spent several days searching. Gradually I built up my library again. There were not many books, but there was one I had read at the time of the competitive entrance exam for the Moroccan Civil Service Academy (I flunked it by one point): Camus's *The Stranger.* Ah, what joy, what delight to rediscover those pages where every word, every phrase, is carefully thought out! For a

solid month, I recited *The Stranger* to my companions. I remembered poor Abdelkader dying because no one told him
stories anymore. With Camus, I felt at ease and was only too
happy to recall certain passages. This conferred on them an immense importance that went far beyond the story of the crime.
A novel related in a dungeon, in the presence of death, cannot
have the same meaning, the same consequences, as it would
when read on the beach or in a meadow, in the shade of cherry
trees.

My eyes had imprinted the text. I read it without stopping, as
though it were appearing before me on a blackboard or a pro-
jection screen. Every now and then, someone would shout,
"Repeat that, repeat it, please, say that paragraph again!"

I would repeat it, slowly, separating the words, allowing time
for the syllables to change into images. "The sun beat almost
straight down on the sand, and the glare from the water was
unbearable." I emphasized the words "sun" and "glare." I
thought that by repeating that sentence I would flood our dungeon with unbearable light. I continued: "The sunlight was
now hammering down. It shattered to pieces on the sand and
the sea." I said "the sand" and "the sea" particularly distinctly,
and repeated them. I went on: "After a moment, I went back to
the beach and started walking . . . There was the same red
glare. The sea panted on the sand with all the rapid, muffled
breathing of its lapping waves. I walked slowly toward the
rocks and felt my head swelling in the sunlight." Now, there, I
wasn't sure. Was it "my head" or "my temples"? It was only a
detail, and I asked Camus in advance to forgive me if I was
mangling one of his sentences.

Everyone had his own way of responding to this recital. I had
my personal stock of images, too. It was full to bursting. I had
to empty it out a bit, pour a few images onto the ground and
watch them glimmer briefly before they died. Reading brought
new images. They piled up, stuck to one another, melted together, then erased themselves: the sun, the beach, the sweat,

the blood, the bodies riddled with bullets, the sea, and I, knocking "on misfortune's door."

Fighting back against the darkness, I was like a well of seething words. I could not keep still. Reading and rereading were not enough to keep us busy anymore. The story had to be invented, rewritten, adapted to our solitude. The Stranger was ideal for this kind of exercise. Without the urgency of our struggle to save our very being from degradation, I would never have dared to touch this novel. I took liberties with Camus and I re-created Meursault's story. I switched the roles: Raymond, Masson, and Meursault would be quietly playing the flute, one summer Sunday, when some Arabs, immigrants, would attack them. There would be the same sun, the same light, and above all the same absurdity. As in the novel, only the French would have names. The others, the Arabs, including the one who would shoot Meursault four times, would remain nameless.

I soon realized that Camus's novel was tamper-resistant. I returned to my usual recitation until I was so tired I could no longer read the sentences running through my head. They were vanishing into a kind of fog. I informed my companions that the recital was over for the moment. Then, like a distant murmur, I heard someone repeating the opening of the book.

"Mama died today. Or maybe yesterday, I'm not sure. I received a telegram from the nursing home: 'Mother deceased. Funeral tomorrow. Deepest sympathy.' The meaning isn't clear. Maybe it was yesterday."

Then I heard a different voice.

"Today, I am going to die. Or maybe tomorrow, I don't know. My mother will not receive a telegram from Tazmamart, or any deepest sympathy. The meaning isn't clear. Maybe it was yesterday."

Another voice.

"Then, I shot four more times at a motionless body, into which the bullets vanished without a trace. As if I were giving four brief knocks on misfortune's door."

22

Rebuilding things as if the dungeon were not our last home. That was fighting back: endlessly, patiently, stubbornly, never giving in, not thinking of the executioners, or of the one who had planned even the slightest detail of the way death would arrive slowly, so slowly, down to ripping out our souls teardrop by teardrop, so that agony would possess our bodies and grind us only gradually into extinction.

Rebuilding things with your mind, avoiding the snares of memory. After so many years, I no longer feared my distant— very distant—past. It now belonged to a stranger. When I remembered, I was not afraid of dying of nostalgia anymore. I did not even need to burn or rearrange any images. I had grown stronger than the temptation of tears that led toward a different tunnel. I looked at my memories as if they belonged to someone else. I was an intruder, a voyeur. I wanted to see the face of my former fiancée once more; I had no trouble finding it. In the sunshine, in the port of Essaouira, she is sitting on a wobbly chair; someone, who must have been me at the age of nineteen, smiles and pushes the chair with his foot to make it tip over. She laughs. So does he. She wants a kiss. He doesn't dare kiss her in public, on the terrace of the harbor café. A strolling photographer takes their picture and tells them, "Tomorrow, same time, same place." She stands up. He follows her with his eyes, sees the light gleaming on her long hair. Afraid that she will go away, that he will lose her, he runs, catches her by the waist, and the two of them fall down on the sand. Children laugh at the sight. The lovers get up again. She checks her watch. "I have to go, my father can't bear not finding me at the house when he comes home. See you tomorrow, same time, same place!" Her lover is sad. He walks along the sand, alone. The sun sets.

I felt nothing when I saw those images again. They passed

the time but did not concern me. That man in love—I could not
even identify with him, it was beyond me now. "So that's fine!"
I decided, and indulged myself with other recollections, where
I could only be a stranger dazzled and stunned by what he
thought he saw happening to him. Passing the time! That was
our main occupation, apparently. Time, however, did not
move. This amused me and made no sense. Like boredom. We
had become creatures of boredom, packages stuffed with boredom. Boredom smelled like cemeteries when the stones are wet.
It skulked around us, chewed on our eyelids, scratched our
skin, and burrowed into our bellies.

I knew that my precious memories had gone traveling, over
to the other side of the night; perhaps they were waiting for me
to get out of the hole so they could return to their places. For
the moment they were far away, set aside, and viewing them
again would not hurt me. I could not overdo this, or expect too
much of them in the state I was in. Taking this small liberty, I allowed myself to play with them, and even to anticipate what
turn events would take. My fiancée was not my fiancée anymore. I had no right to shut her up inside a house. I had lib-
erated her. How would she discover this? I quickly became
convinced that our families and dear ones considered us dead.
Only my mother must still be hoping to see me alive once more.
A mother is never wrong about the life or death of her child.
Later, I would discover that strangers used to come knocking
on her door and whisper to her sadly, as if they were telling her
a secret, "Your son is dead. He was executed two months ago:
tied to a tree, blindfolded, and shot by a firing squad. You
know, Madame, we're not allowed to tell you this, but we're all
Muslims and we should show compassion. We belong to God
and to Him we will return!"

They would disappear, wrapped in their brown woolen
djellabas, without giving her time to ask any questions.

Other men would come to claim the opposite, smiling and
confident: "Your son is alive, he's well, he's constructing a

mountain with other officers. It's very hush-hush. You mustn't talk about it . . ."

Luckily, my mother believed solely in her own intuitions.

I would receive messages from her. Presentiments. I knew that she knew. My fiancée did not know me well enough to be connected to me by our thoughts. After the shock of the prison in Kenitra, where my fiancée had twice come to visit me, she understood that a life with me was not in her future. She had cried. Tears of farewell. And then there was the last look, the one you give someone on his deathbed. She stared at me, tears pouring down her cheeks, then turned and walked quickly and resolutely away. I had forbidden myself to feel any pain or regret. Everything I had known and experienced before July 10, 1971, would no longer count, no longer torment me or invade my cell.

In time, I had grown calmer, and above all closed to everything that might let in the wind of the past. I was able to play games and even to entertain myself. I spent several days finding a husband for my fiancée. I wanted him tall, at least as tall as I had been when I was first imprisoned; I envisioned a blond, different from me, perhaps even a European, an educated man, a professor of literature or an artist. I felt like concocting a wonderful life for her, a man who would offer her everything I hadn't had time to give her. He would take her to Greece, Italy, Andalusia, to visit the Prado in Madrid, the Louvre in Paris. He would buy her books they would read in bed together. He would introduce her to the theater, to classical music. He would make her a Moroccan woman different from all others, he would make her dream, make her forget the time we'd had together.

And I had to forget that part of my life, too. What right had I to choose her husband? Maybe she had already found him and they were living in perfect harmony in Marrakech or Casablanca. Perhaps they fought a lot and in her unhappiness she thought of me, of us? No, I hoped she didn't think about me. Ever. And I was not to think anymore about the trembling beauty of beings and things, or the softness of a summer night, or the transparence of a dream caressing the half-closed eyes of a child.

I went no further, convinced I had become a book no one would ever open.

23

We never learned much about Sebban, who joined us early in the 1980s. The guards brought him in during our midday meal. He was tall, quite tall, a big guy with a matte complexion and not one hair on his smooth skull. He said nothing, replied to neither our calls nor our questions. The next day, I was chosen to explain our routine and the few rules we had established for ourselves. I asked him his name several times. After a silence he replied, "Sebban. Call me Sebban."

"Where are you from?"

Silence.

"Why are you here?

Silence.

"Listen, Sebban. We're organized, here. We alternately learn the Koran or listen to stories. One day a week, Omar tells us about Paris. He spent a month there when he was twenty. The afternoon is devoted to group discussions. For a month now we've been debating colonialism. You're free to participate in these activities. Silence at night is of primary importance. After supper, quiet must be observed, because we have to rest. Yes, even here, we need to rest. The walls between the cells are thin. You hear everything, the sighs and the snoring. If you accept this schedule, say so, or if you don't feel like talking, knock twice on your cell door."

When I heard the two knocks, I was relieved. He spent his nights doing gymnastics, and everyone could hear him breathing heavily as he performed his push-ups. In the morning, he slept. A few of us tried to get him to talk, without success. After two months, I obtained—with some difficulty—permission to see Sebban. I had explained the problem to a guard, who was as eager as I was to penetrate the mystery of that man. He even told me, "All I know is that he belonged to the royal guard. He must have done something dreadful to wind up here. Maybe he was disrespectful to a princess . . . Who knows!"

I had all morning to talk with him. When the guard opened his door and shined his flashlight on him, I saw right away that he was feverish. His lips were quivering and sweat trickled down his forehead. I gave up any idea of asking him the same questions we had tried when he first arrived. He waited for the guard to leave before stammering out a few words. Keeping his right arm tucked behind his back, he told me in rudimentary French, "I like sport. Here I all the time do sport."

"Is it true you were in the royal guard?"

"I not know."

"What are you hiding behind your back?"

"Nothing. *Walou* (nothing) . . ."

"Why are you holding your arm behind your back?"

"Because. *Walou* . . ."

"Well, show it to me. May I see it?"

After a few moments, he whirled around and said to me, "Look."

"I'm sorry, there's never any light here, let's wait for the guard to come back with his flashlight. In the meantime, tell me what it is."

"It hurts, hurts a lot."

"Since when?"

"Oh, since second week I arrived."

When the guard came to get me, he shined his flashlight on Sebban's back, and I saw a broken arm with the bones of the elbow protruding from gangrened flesh. Sebban turned around again to face the door.

"How long do you think he's got?" the guard asked me.

"I don't know. Unless the cockroaches gobble him up before the gangrene can spread throughout his body."

Which is what happened. He was eaten alive by thousands of roaches and other insects that had deserted our cells for his. The guards were afraid to open his door. They would ask if he was still alive, and then we would hear a kick or two against his door. By day, the smell of death hovered around the cell block. At night, a screech owl began a mournful cry, a sign that the end was near. In the beginning, we had paid no attention, but with time we learned that after such a song, a dying man would not last two weeks. It was Karim who had first noticed this.

I called to Sebban several times.

"If you hear me, say anything at all, or bang on the door."

After an hour, I was sure he was dead. The next day the guards opened the cell and shined a light inside, then slammed the door shut and ran out, cursing.

They returned that afternoon, wearing protective gloves and face masks. They were afraid to touch him. They offered to let me out if I would help them.

The gangrene had spread rapidly. I saw worms come out of the soles of his feet. There were so many cockroaches it was hard to clear them off the body and get it into the plastic bag. We absolutely had to kill these thousands of roaches. A guard brought a poison used by the army against grasshoppers, a powder so dangerous that I had to wear a mask and gloves. In a few minutes, all the roaches had fallen to the floor in clumps from the walls and ceiling. The guard brought a shovel and a wheelbarrow to gather them up.

Sebban's death rid us of the cockroaches. I had kept a little powder, which I sprinkled along the thresholds of all the cells. The guard told me that this was against the rules.

"If we don't kill them, they'll eat us all within a few days. Well, here death is supposed to take its time. Maybe I am acting against the rules, but I'm being consistent. Death, fine—but by inches!"

"You sound like the Kmandar!"

Yes, I had assimilated his spirit and technique. For the first time, the guard saluted me.

24

Every group has its bastard. At the Military Academy, we had a snitch, a coward, and a pain in the ass. It was only natural that one of these three would end up in the dungeon with us.

There is some vulgarity hidden in everyone. The man who had more than his share, the most unbearable prisoner in the hole, was Achar. A being at the limit of humanity. An animal aping a man. Achar was not only crude, he was vicious. At first he disgusted me, but then, I changed my attitude: Achar did not deserve any feeling at all from me beyond indifference. I would recognize his existence only when absolutely necessary. Indifference was not the absence but the repudiation of all emotion.

Achar was an incorrigible pain in the ass. He was older than the rest of us, a quartermaster sergeant. He was illiterate, coarse, brutal, and glad of it. He had been a soldier in Indochina, and he invented or exaggerated experiences from that episode. To him the Vietnamese were "the Chinese," whom he spoke of in racist and insulting terms.

He had become involved in the coup d'état by accident when he sneaked into one of the trucks leaving Ahermemou. He had wanted to take advantage of the ride to settle a quarrel with a cousin who was a grocer in Rabat. We had learned all about that in a hurry, because he spent the first few years of our imprisonment cursing this cousin when he got up in the morning and when he went to bed at night, praying the man would die a horrible death.

"May God crush you under a tank and make you pick up your guts with your own hands and take a long time to die."

Or, "May God send you breakbone fever from Indochina to drive you crazy and make you eat the fingers right off your hands, one by one."

*   *   *

Achar was evil. Through him I discovered envy and jealousy, two sicknesses rather common in everyday life but that had no place in our dungeon. Achar brought them along with him, however, allowing them to develop and poison our meager existence.

His cell was across from mine. His favorite pastime was to interrupt our discussions or spend the night humming just to drive us nuts. We had no way of disciplining him. I realized that we had to include him in everything we did, in spite of his lack of education. Abandoning the study group that was making fairly good progress in learning the Koran, I decided to teach him the holy book myself.

"Why are you in the group and not me?" he complained. "I'm a man, too, a good Muslim, I've had experience—the Chinese remember me!"

He had trouble concentrating and particular difficulty pronouncing words properly. I had to say each syllable distinctly. He would repeat things after me, then shout out his hatred of Islam and the Koran. For that, I would punish him: I stopped speaking to him until he said he was sorry. I would have him pray. I felt that he was raging against his own ignorance. After a month, he was able to recite the Fatiha, the first sura, without any mistakes. He really wanted to join our group and to be considered one of us, but he could not control his envy.

The day the guard allowed me to visit Sebban, he became furious.

"Why does the guard talk to you, why does he pick you and not me? I'm older, I'm the vet'ran. How do you get special treatment? Hey, what do you give him? Why you and not me? Huh? Hey, answer me, I'm an Indochinese vet'ran. I know them, the Chinese. You, you're like them. You don't talk. You're slipp'ry. Everything's done *men tiht el tiht,* on the sly."

I did not answer. I let him stew. At the end of the day, he asked me, "How about doing the Sura of the Cow?*"

"Not this evening. Tomorrow. It's time to be quiet now. Stop talking and try to think by following the rhythm of your breathing. Learn to appreciate silence. Tell yourself that being quiet is restful for yourself and the others, especially the others. We really need silence. It can replace the light we miss so much."

"All right. You're not angry at me? You'll tell me what Sebban said to you? He's dead, so you can speak. You promise, hey, Monsieur Slipp'ry?"

"Achar, shut up, or else no Koran tomorrow."

He fell silent, but I could hear him muttering before he went to sleep. Sometimes he dreamed out loud, waking me with his cries and babbling. When I told him about this the next morning, he would swear on his mother's head that it wasn't him.

One day, the guard withheld his food. Achar was outraged and claimed that I was behind this punishment. I tried to explain that I'd had nothing to do with it, but he yelled and insulted everybody and finally prayed to put the evil eye on me. Where we were, the evil eye or a wicked spell, black magic, talismans and incantations—they couldn't touch us. In that sense, we were out of reach. So I laughed. That drove him up a wall. When the guard appeared the next day with his ration of starch, Achar asked if he could have a little extra.

"You're fat enough already!" the guard replied.

Without his stubbornness and his frequent lousy moods, Achar would have been an ordinary prisoner. The rest of our survival together taught me that we could endure even meanness and bad feelings among ourselves in that hole where we had been left to rot.

25

One evening when I was finishing my prayers (not those of that day, but prayers I had neglected to say when I was a free man), the little sparrow of Marrakech, the bird of my childhood, the sacred bird called Tebebt or Lfqéra, came to visit me. Later I would learn that this bird was a striolated bunting: the head, neck, and breast are of a uniform gray, and the rest of the plumage is chestnut or reddish brown. For a while I had confused it with the chaffinch because their songs are so much alike. At the time, however, I amused myself by trying to guess its name in French and the color of its plumage. This bird alighted in the hole that served as an air vent for the cell and sang for a good fifteen minutes. Naturally, I fed him some bread crumbs moistened with water. After eating, he sang again, then flew away. He must have had his nest in a tree nearby. When he returned, he landed on the main vent and sang; acting as a lookout, he changed his tune whenever he observed any movement outside the prison, so the arrival of the guards was always announced by Tebebt.

I can still remember his different songs, which I soon learned to distinguish. One day, when he twittered in a quick, staccato manner, I didn't realize what that rhythm meant . . . Tebebt was welcoming the rain! We'd had no way of knowing what the sky was like, but thanks to this bunting, we were getting a weather report. Our bird was the one who alerted us when a sandstorm was coming, warning us through the way he sang that something was brewing. With time and experience, I became skilled in decoding his different songs. The guards were surprised whenever we said, "That was some downpour!" Or, "How was the storm?"

These distinctions took a few months to imprint themselves on my memory. I learned, for example, that when he changed his morning song, he wanted to tell us that one of the guards had gone off on leave.

I remarked one day to the two guards on duty, "How come the other guy went on leave and not you two?"

"How do you know that?"

"I just do."

They said we were djinns, unholy people who must have made a pact with the devil.

Tebebt had become my companion, my friend. When he landed on the edge of my air vent, I fancied that I spied the sparkle in his eyes, and in spite of the darkness, I would talk to him in a low voice, so as not to make Achar jealous. I would tell the bird about my day and ask him not to come by during prayers. Curiously, when he did come inside, he waited patiently for the end of prayers. At the words *Assalam alaïkum,* he knew that I had finished and would be turning my attention to him.

Achar the Envious asked me one day, "What's going on with this bird? Why does he come to your cell but not mine? You've trained him so he won't sing for me! Why this contempt? Why this unkindness? I deserve to have a sparrow brighten up my crappy days, too! I need a fucking bird to pay attention to my loneliness, my misery. What do you give him to make him love you? Come on, tell me what your trick is!"

"Calm down, Achar," I told him. "This bird is a sign of God's mercy. He is the messenger of hope for me—I who have refused to believe in hope! He comes to me by chance. Maybe someday he'll visit you. Don't be jealous of a little bitty sparrow! That's ridiculous. Turn to prayer. I counted up the number of days from before when I should have been saying my five daily prayers, and there are a lot of them. From when I was fifteen to when I was twenty-two, I stopped believing and praying. Now I give God six days of prayers from before, plus that day's prayers. It's like a credit: I'm paying back for my lateness, my forgetfulness, my straying from the path. I'm taking stock of myself as I was a long time ago. I'm not proud of the man I was at twenty! So I believe in God, I believe in Mohammed, in Jesus, and in Moses. I believe in the superiority of faith. I believe in the present, but I no longer have a past. Each day that passes is a day that dies without a trace, without a sound, without color. Every morning I am a newborn baby. I even consider myself to be like Tebebt, who is a sensitive sparrow, quite astute and above suspicion. I understand the language of sparrows better than I do that of humans. Tebebt makes me travel and accompanies me on my flights toward spirituality. His lightness, his fragility, the sweetness of his song, the nuances of his messages are a great help to me. After the last evening prayer, when the cold gnaws at my bones, when pain racks my arms and hands, when calling for help or screaming is useless, I remember Tebebt's song. I reconstruct it from memory, and play it over and over in my head, until my suffering has loosened its grip. That, Achar, is why the sparrow visits me. Between myself and him, there is a bond. It's as slender as a silken thread, like a single hair. This bond is the only thing I accept from the outside, because I know this bird was born for me. He was sent by a mother's distress or the will of God. Good night, Achar!"

After that, Achar began to pay attention. He asked me to teach him the five prayers, admitting, to his great shame, that the army had been his only family and that religion was never mentioned in the barracks. He told me that during the war in Indochina, he had called on Allah when he went into battle.

But Achar never lost his arrogance and his surly disposition.

26

In my life from before, not only did I sleep badly, but I dreamed very little. During the first months in prison, I lost both sleep and dreams. After I broke with the past and hope, I slept normally, except for nights of piercing cold when we had to stay awake to keep from freezing to death. And I dreamed. All my nights were packed with dreams. Some of them marked me, and I remembered them. Others left me with a vague impression that was rarely disagreeable.

I was not alone in crowding my sleep with dreams, but I must have been the only one to dream of the three prophets.

With Moses, I had a long political discussion. We were facing each other, he sitting on a throne, I on the ground. I told him that the inequality of men was a source of injustice. He listened but did not speak to me.

Jesus did not say anything either. He came by from time to time, with sad eyes and outstretched arms.

With Mohammed, I didn't see his face, but I sensed his presence, all made of light. I heard a voice—deep, grave, distant—echoing in my head as though an old wise man were murmuring in my ear, counseling patience.

O you who suffer,
know that patience is a virtue of faith,
know also that it is a gift from God.
Remember the prophet Job,
the one who endured everything;
he is given in example by God, and called worthy.
O Muslim, you are not forgotten despite the darkness
  and the walls;
know that patience is the path

and the key to deliverance, after all,
and well you know that God is with those who have
*   patience!*

After those dreams, I felt peaceful. They reassured me. I was on the path of truth and justice. I had no need to fill my heart with hope. God had not abandoned me. Death could come; as for suffering, I tried to consider it as a minor affair, something to be overcome. Powerful, unshakable, such was my faith. It was detached, by which I mean pure. It gave me a strength and a will I had not demanded of it. I told no one about my dreams of prophets. They belonged to me. However, there was a dream that made me uneasy: the one about the couscous man.

In this dream, there are many of us outside the door of the mosque. We are hungry and clothed in rags. It is very hot. We don't dare enter the mosque because we have no water for the ritual ablutions. People pass by without seeing or speaking to us. One of us gets up suddenly and runs off. We watch him go, but something invisible prevents us from moving. A few moments later he returns bearing a large dish of mutton couscous with seven vegetables. He sets it down. We all crowd around it and eat with our hands. He, however, stands off to one side, without eating or speaking. Watching us, he backs slowly away.

This dream had finally taken on a precise meaning: the death of one among us. But I was not the only prisoner to have premonitory dreams. When I would talk about mine in the morning, the others would mention theirs. Wakrine said it was a bad sign to dream about corn: "A man is standing by the side of the road, next to a peasant who's roasting ears of corn and who gives him one for free, saying, 'Here, eat, it's good, one for the road.' As the man walks away, he sees an acquaintance, but the fellow goes by without greeting him. He realizes that the other man did not recognize him."

*   *   *

Abbass's dreams were even more explicit. A party: laughter, light, lots of sunshine, and in the center a huge cage full of pigeons and doves. A white hand comes down from the sky, slips between the bars of the cage, and grabs a pigeon before vanishing among the clouds.

The dreams we were comparing centered on a single premonition. During the same period, the odor of death entered the dungeon. It drifted around, lurking near certain cells, until it settled on one of them. At night, screech owls gave their gloomy cries, announcing in their own way that someone would disappear. Their dirges sometimes lasted for two weeks, and ceased after the funeral.

We all paid attention to the birds' messages. Only Achar had trouble following what was happening and grumbled, angry at us for being ahead of him. We alerted the guards: time to get the plastic bag and quicklime ready. Time to dig a grave. They were usually reluctant to make such preparations.

"We're guards, not grave diggers!"

"I can't help it," I would tell them. "Our dreams are unequivocal: someone is going to die. I don't know which of us death will carry off. Me, I'm ready, but I don't feel it's my turn. If the pain in my spine becomes unbearable, you can kill me, it'll be a relief."

"In your dreams! As if we'd be so kind! Here, being kind is forbidden. That's just how it is. You should know that, after all this time!"

"But we're in the same boat . . ."

"No, you're mistaken. We are loyal and honest soldiers. It's an honor for us to be chosen by the army to carry out this task."

"We're all from the same family!"

"Not on your life! If you keep asking for it, you're going to get it!"

"Go ahead!"

"Never!"

I would laugh, and Achar would fume, because he felt left out.

On at least one night every winter, the guards went crazy.

We'd be sleeping when they would burst in, flashlights shining, clubs and submachine guns slung across their shoulders. They would be quite upset, intent on putting an end to some imaginary uproar.

"You've got to stop making noise, grunting like wild pigs, cackling like djinns—cut it out, or we'll let in the rats!"

We would be fast asleep when they awakened us. We'd ask them to leave us alone, swearing that no one had said anything, or laughed, or shouted. It was no use. They were convinced that we had been partying or plotting revolution. After they left, we couldn't help it, we'd be in stitches, telling ourselves, well, they've gone insane. And then they would return, more agitated than before, hammering on our doors with their clubs. The racket was deafening.

"If you're possessed by djinns, if you've made a pact with the devil, we'll beat you down and pound you to pieces. So, enough of this circus!"

We had no desire to argue or prove to them that there were no djinns in the dungeon. If you ask me, if djinns exist, they would stay away from that hole where evil had already done its work.

On other nights, we would hear gunshots, and find out later that they'd thought they had seen a shadow and had opened fire, following orders to shoot at anything suspicious.

They blazed away at phantoms, especially when there was a full moon or their nerves were on edge. The next morning, they would report to the Kmandar, who in turn would notify headquarters in Rabat about the incident. Shots fired in error. Nervous tension. Adverse effect of the full moon on guards, and so on. This entertained us but did not make our survival less grueling. Achar, however, was always pleased.

"That's fine," he would say. "We're not the only ones seeing things. They're going around the bend, too. That's good for my morale."

One day they came and sprinkled disinfectant around the dungeon. Then they returned with incense, which was supposed to chase away the djinns. This really tickled me. They said several incantations along the lines of, "May God protect us from those who have made a pact with Chaïtane, who have eaten from his hands and who bear evil in their eyes! May God the All-powerful put an end to the wicked work of Satan and his disciples. May He give us the strength and vision to triumph over his misdeeds and may He allow us to go away on leave soon so we can forget the madness that threatens us in this eternally desolate land!"

Then I piped up with different prayers: "I appeal to God to preserve us from Satan the Furious!"

"أَعُـوذ بِالله مِن الشَّيطان الرَّجِيـم"

My companions repeated this after me, while Ustad Gharbi recited the Koran. The recitation frightened the guards, who knew they were being ridiculous and ran out of the dungeon. I heard later that this "exorcism" had been their own idea, the only initiative they ever took during my eighteen years in the dungeon, and the Kmandar had not been informed of it. He never set foot in the hole but knew about everything that happened there. In the beginning, when one of us was seriously ill, we would beg the guards to let the Kmandar know. When they dared report to him, for example, that "Number 6 is very sick," he would scream at them.

"Don't ever come tell me so-and-so is sick! Don't come except to tell me he's dead, so I can keep my files up to date. Got that? I don't ever want to hear the word 'sick.' Now—get out!"

This Kmandar who never showed himself was an enigma. One day, just to get some attention, Achar claimed he used to know the Kmandar. Without challenging him, we decided to describe the man, or at least to say how we imagined him.

"He's short, squat, and ugly."

"He has a mustache, makes him look manly."

"He's got bad breath."

"He's illiterate, can't read or write anything but short, simple reports."

"He's thin, his face is seamed, his eyes are deep set and they stare at you coldly."

"He's definitely got some kind of physical defect."

"He has no family."

"He has no trouble sleeping."

"He's incorruptible."

"He's very disciplined and doesn't eat seafood."

"He's obedient, like a dog trained to kill his victims, cut their throats, drink their blood, and eat their livers."

"He never has any doubts."

"To have doubts, you have to think—and he never thinks!"

"He must have an incurable disease."

"I bet he's modeling himself on Oufkir."

"He's all that," interrupted Achar, "plus something you haven't a clue about. He's a cannibal. He likes to eat human flesh. He's a gourmand, he prefers young boys. If they've transferred him here, it's to get him away from Rabat and also to punish him. But for him it's not a punishment—it's an honor to carry out the orders of his superiors. He loves to obey and always overdoes it. If you saw him in the street, you wouldn't notice him."

"You're right, Achar. Monsters don't wear on their faces all the cruelty they have inside them. The Kmandar must be a good soldier serving the army and the top brass."

I later learned that this Kmandar was the brutal and cynical product of the French colonial army, the one from Indochina, the one that served in Morocco under General Boyer de La Tour, whom the Berbers called Moha ou La Tour, who had noticed and trained the young Oufkir and presented him at the palace.

The Kmandar belonged to Oufkir's generation. He, too, was a lieutenant in the French army. He had been promoted, had joined the Royal Armed Forces, and had been an instructor at the Military Academy. He had not been chosen at random to run the dungeon. He had been of particular service to the army and the police. He was a kind of silent, stone-cold killer.

There are Kmandars everywhere in this world. They have the faces of men but their minds and bodies have been carefully drained of all humanity. They have stripped themselves of everything that is human, the way others accept the shedding of their own blood. No scruples. No misgivings.

The Kmandar played his part with frightening simplicity and ease. He had completely assumed the role of someone who delivers death with calculated slowness and meticulous doses of pain. That's all he was. Full of that mission and that desire instilled in him by others. Full of pus with which to infect his victims, his belly swollen with a mindless hatred, his eyes jaundiced by the yellow blood of submission to his superiors.

The Kmandar liked to think he was the Kmandar, and hid away, playing on the surviving prisoners' nerves, howling all alone like a rabid hyena. That brute was an abyss unto himself.

I never thought about him.

28

Although I was able to struggle against discouragement, banish the Kmandar from my thoughts, and understand that I needed to wrestle with myself instead of fighting him and his ghosts, I sometimes wondered what vitality was sustaining my body and spirit.

Suffering did not choose my path for me—I did, before and beyond all suffering. I had to overcome my doubts, my failures, and most of all, the illusions nourished by every human being. How? By letting them wither away inside me. I no longer trusted those images that falsified reality. It is a weakness to mistake one's feelings for reality, to foster a lie that begins and ends in oneself, and to consider this an accomplishment.

Now, to make headway through this desert, I had to break free of everything. I understood that only a mind that can shake off all bonds can lead us to the subtle peace I will call ecstasy.

Number 5, Abdelmalek, was a nice guy. He never complained. Achar used to badger him and envied him his serenity.

"Abdelmalek, aren't you ever in pain?! You want to make us believe you're a superman, like my neighbor across the way. But I think you're hiding something. You're a traitor with your silence, you withdraw from the group. Everyone is sick in here. No one's healthy. You're the only guy who doesn't have to suffer like we do? What the hell do you take us for!"

I had to intervene at this point.

"Achar, be quiet, leave him alone. Respect his wishes."

"Oh naturally, you're the same as he is. You're stuck-up too, a real he-man, nothing bothers you. I'm onto your game. I'm not stupid."

"Stop it, Achar, or we'll quarantine you."

"No! Not that! It'd kill me . . . But, please, tell your friend to talk to me, just a little bit."

"I don't need to ask him. If he feels like talking to you, he will. If he keeps quiet, it's because he has his reasons."

"Okay, I'm shutting up! All right . . . I'm bored! How do you keep from being bored?"

"I think, I pray, I recite the suras of the Koran to myself, I try to come up with stories to tell you all. That's what I do."

After a moment of silence, he asked, "Can you help me recite the Sura of the Cow?"

"Not now. It's time for Fouad to give us our English lesson."

Abdelmalek no longer participated in our activities. He was absent. I was becoming worried but did not dare disturb him.

The guards noticed he wasn't eating his beans anymore but was keeping the bread. He had made a bag from one of his 1936 blankets and was stashing the bread inside it. He would let the bread get very hard, break it into pieces that he crushed with his heel, moisten the crumbs, and swallow them. It was his single daily meal. He was eating just these crumbs of stale bread that had spent several days in his bag.

We did not know it, but he had chosen his way of dying. When I called to him, he would tell me that everything was fine and that deliverance was nigh. I found this funny, and asked him if he had found a way to escape.

"Yes, but this time they won't catch me."

He was, in fact, the only one of us who had ever tried to get away. One morning at the beginning of our imprisonment in the dungeon, when the guards opened his cell to put the bread and coffee inside, he had pushed his way past them, knocked over the tin pot of coffee, and run out the door, which had been left ajar. The screeching guards gave chase and caught him in the middle of the courtyard, where they gave him a beating.

"You dirty bastard! You almost got us killed! What did we

ever do to make you screw us like that? It's lucky we nabbed you—the guards up in the watchtowers have orders to shoot anything that moves!"

When they returned him to his cell, they read us the riot act.

"If you try to break out, you'll be shot down—and us with you!"

The failure of this attempt put an end to all thoughts of escape. Abdelmalek never really recovered. He died in atrocious agony, which lasted several days. After he was removed by the guards, I collected his clothing, his blanket, and his bag, which was still full of bread. When I opened it in front of a guard with a flashlight, I was appalled: there were more cockroaches inside it than bread. They had laid their eggs among the bread crumbs. Poor Abdelmalek could not see what he was eating. He was poisoned by thousands of roach eggs.

Achar was deeply affected by this death and sorry he had taunted Abdelmalek a few weeks before his end.

29

Karim, our talking clock, our calendar, our beacon in the darkness, was getting tired. He gave the year and the month, but not the day or the hour. The machine was running down, the memory was wearing out. I knew approximately what time it was, and at his request, I took on the job.

We had been in that dungeon now for thirteen years. More than half of us had died. We still had the same guards, who were assigned to us for life. Often there were birds; some sang, others informed us about doings in the courtyard or what the weather was up to.

We had established a certain routine in hell. The guards were frequently in a bad mood. Some of them complained about the loneliness. I had noticed that Sergeant M'Fadel, the senior guard, would sometimes stop by the cell on my left to speak with Wakrine in Tamazight,* just making small talk. One day, M'Fadel kept his voice low—they were whispering. I did not say anything, but I figured they were probably from the same hometown. I discovered later that not only were they cousins by marriage, but their families were related by a kind of pact called *tata* by the Berbers. I never learned the origin of this word. The Indochina veterans used it in the barracks to mean a round hut in which soldiers were placed under close arrest for a few hours.

To the Berbers, however, it meant something else entirely: for complex reasons, a given family pledges allegiance to another family or tribe, placing itself under their protection, even under their blessing. The ties become stronger and, above all, sacred. Moral assistance, material aid, and absolute solidarity are owed to the members of a family known to be *tata*.

I do not know how they recognized one another. It took Wakrine and M'Fadel years to discover they were bound by the laws of *tata*.

A few weeks after I had heard him whispering with M'Fadel, Wakrine knocked twice on the wall between our two cells.

"Can you write a letter to my wife?"

I was amazed.

"A letter? But, have you got what I'd need, some paper and a pencil?"

"I'll have them soon. I think there's a chance of getting a letter through to my wife. It's not very certain yet."

"How would you get paper and a pencil? You know as well as I do those are precious things and absolutely forbidden in the hole."

"Listen, I'll explain it to you, but for the moment, just tell me if you'll help me out with this. You know I've forgotten the alphabet. I can't read anymore. It's my illness. But you've kept all your brains. I can't remember words now."

"Sure I'll help you. But be very careful."

"Of course. M'Fadel is my cousin. Actually, not exactly. My wife is his wife's cousin. I think there's a sort of agreement between our two families. I'll explain what kind to you some day. He hasn't the right to speak, but I believe he'll agree to smuggle out my letter. For that he'll have to wait for his next leave and especially for a change in the guard who frisks the soldiers when they go."

And that's how after three months of waiting, of secret meetings, and risks, Wakrine was able to slip out his open cell door to come slide under mine a small sheet of paper and a pencil stub. I swept my hand over the floor and quietly picked them up. I was delirious with joy, incredibly excited, and trying hard not to reveal it. I brought the pencil to my lips—yes, I kissed that tiny bit of wood with the pencil lead inside. Then I handled the paper, delicately; it was rough, but who cared about the quality of this paper that I already saw as a thin ray of light in our darkness?

First I composed the letter in my head. How should I begin? Should I write indirectly, or just blurt out the truth? I kept erasing things in my mind and starting over. Wakrine urged me on.

"Tell my wife I'm alive and that she should give medicines to M'Fadel."

"Yes, but we must use this chance to alert the other families about our fate . . ."

"I trust you. But don't forget, M'Fadel's taking a huge risk! Write ordinary stuff."

So, after thinking about this for four days, I cut the paper in half and wrote the following.

I am well. We are in Tazmamart. No light. Give M'Fadel medicines for pain. Wakrine.

From that moment on, and thanks to that scrap of paper, our survival would undergo momentous changes. I myself did not want to write to anyone, since I had decided, from the beginning, that I had neither family nor fiancée.

Five more years were to go by, five years of doubt during which hope returned—a hope that went against my principles. I absolutely had to mistrust it, and to survive in that hell by resisting death with the means at hand: willpower and spirituality.

M'Fadel carried the piece of paper to Wakrine's wife and gave it to her without a word. Since she could not read, she showed it to a woman whose son had disappeared. This was how a young man studying in France learned the whereabouts of his older brother, Omar, our Number 18. The woman had a daughter who was a pharmacist, who gave M'Fadel some medicines, mostly analgesics and anti-inflammatories, along with a tidy sum of money.

I realized immediately that M'Fadel had been bribed—even

if he did act out of tribal solidarity—when he came looking for Wakrine a few months later to ask him if he needed any medicines. Even in hell corruption works miracles! For the first time, I saw the virtue in it. To think that corruption would help save a few lives! Other scraps of paper found their way out of the hole, and M'Fadel was growing rich. Omar's brother contacted Christine, an exceptional woman, a human rights activist, a rebellious La Pasionaria who would devote years of her life to exposing the existence of our dungeon and fighting for our release. She did not know us. Yet she concerned herself with our fate as if we were all her brothers. She moved heaven and earth to draw the world's attention to our incarceration, just as she had fought for her husband, whose opinions had landed him in prison in Kenitra. Strangely enough, the Kmandar did not burst into our hole to investigate the source of the leak. He probably suspected the people in Cell Block A, where the discipline was a trifle less harsh. But, after all, the authorities must not have been displeased to have this information come out. In fact, they had every interest in letting the news spread—bringing with it fear and a disguised form of terror. Perhaps M'Fadel had even been assigned to organize these first leaks. If not, why had his compassion waited thirteen years to surface?

As soon as the press started talking about Tazmamart, M'Fadel became afraid. He turned nasty and avoided talking to us. When he went by Wakrine's door, he spat and stammered out some insult in Tamazight.

No one could stop the information from circulating outside. Later, I found out that Christine had contacted Amnesty International and some influential journalists. Now our fate depended not only on the Kmandar but on international opinion as well.

Meanwhile, as though the hope of liberation had provoked this paradox, men were dying.

30

Even today, I am still ashamed of what happened that night in April. I had lost control of myself. It was my turn to give in to a foul mood, anger, and frustration. I had not prayed for two days. I no longer felt like meditating or escaping along the path of the black stone. I had my weaknesses, too, which I had tried to hide or even overcome. And I had succeeded, almost managing to bear the pain that twisted my spine and deformed my hands. But now I no longer wanted to wake up each morning telling myself that the curtains—curtains of cement with permanent folds—had been closed forever, that I had to get up with my head hanging, like someone who expects nothing, and that I should get used to this nothing that seeped from the stones in spite of the letters I wrote for Wakrine.

Perhaps I had been contaminated by the hope hovering around Wakrine and a few others? For the first time, I imagined my liberation. I thought about the sun again. I saw the lights of my childhood once more. Memories I had cast off came flooding back. I saw my mother, dressed all in white, open her arms and hold me close for a long, long time. She wept, and so did I.

Everything I had built up over thirteen years in the dungeon was slowly falling apart. I had to take action, start doing my mental exercises again to get back in spiritual shape. It was at this point, unfortunately, that Lhoucine decided to taunt me. Why did he choose that particular night, a night of doubt and vulnerability, to provoke me?

"You son of a buffoon, you're just a bastard, you're not your father's son, because if he were really your father, would he have publicly disowned you, would he have abandoned you to hell and demanded even worse punishment for you? Answer me, you bastard!"

I should never have replied and let myself get sucked into an

all-out verbal brawl. He had tried to wound me, to strike where
I was most sensitive. Even though I had managed not to be
angry at my father, forgetting him and surviving as if I were a
fatherless orphan, that night I was in a very fragile state. I was
just like everyone else again: helpless, tired, shattered. And I
wanted to hurt Lhoucine, too. I remembered that when we
were in Kenitra, where we had been in adjoining cells, he had
been hospitalized for a heart problem. The doctor who kept
him there for observation took a liking to him, even offering
to arrange for Lhoucine's wife to visit him. At the time, we
were not being held in secret custody yet. We were serving our
ten-year sentences and being treated like ordinary prisoners.
Lhoucine's wife came to see him and they made love. He had
told me about it dozens of times and even admitted to mastur-
bating while he thought about it. From that visit, a child was
born. He heard the news the day before our transfer to Tazmamart. He was ecstatic. I had quickly calculated that it had been
nine months and ten days since the prison hospital visit. I did
not say anything, figuring that the child had been born before
the news reached him. Nevertheless, I used this opening to
strike back at him that night when I was no longer myself.

"Okay, if you want it that way, I'm a bastard! And you,
you're from a good family, your father really is your father, I
don't doubt it. But are you sure you're the father of your son?
Remember, your wife gave birth after nine months and ten
days! Your son isn't a preemie! Whose is he? Somebody took a
poke after you did. Sorry Lhoucine, but you asked for it . . ."

"You son of a bitch! You know my wife is from an honorable
family and that she loves me more than anything. Why are you
making this story up?"

"I'm not making anything up. You're the one who told me
everything. Remember, you even wondered about it, then you
brushed it all away by naming your son Mabrouk, after his
mother!"

"Your father's a pimp!"

"What do I care. You, you're a doormat. At the academy the captain despised you and you never spoke up for yourself!"

"I was obeying orders!"

"How could a cadet agree to run errands for the captain's wife? That's for ordinary soldiers. You haven't a shred of dignity!"

"And you're a stupid jerk! Your father tried to get you promoted to lieutenant but you stayed a cadet, 'cause you're incompetent . . ."

"Screw promotion. Ask yourself why that nice doctor let your wife visit you. You think there was nothing in it for him?"

"My wife isn't like that, you'll see, she'll be waiting for me when I get out. And you, you'll have no one waiting! You're a son of nothing, from nowhere, you whoreson . . ."

"Cuckold!"

"Traitor!"

"Scum!"

"Fag!"

"Jealous!"

"Ass!"

"Jack-off!"

"Son of sin!"

We traded insults all night long. Poor Lhoucine was the one who cracked first and began to cry. I felt like sobbing, too, I was so ashamed of myself, so weary, and so wretched over the pain I had caused him. I felt guilty because he was much more fragile than I was. It didn't matter that I apologized, tried to reassure him, even lied and swore my youngest sister was born three weeks late . . . It was no use, Lhoucine was a broken man. My jeers had finished him off. As for his taunts, they had not really bothered me. They just reminded me of my father and of what he had done. Once more I pictured him at the feet of the king, ridding himself of the unworthy son who had betrayed him and injured his relationship with his sovereign. But Lhoucine was raving. For weeks he did not speak to anyone, calling his wife's name, Mabrouka, day and night. Whenever we recited the Koran, he would mutter, to spoil the harmony of our words. He had become unbearable and was letting himself waste away. When M'Fadel brought medicines, I begged him to let me spend a few hours with Lhoucine in his cell. It was the month of May.

I took him in my arms and gave him some aspirin. He was skeletal. He wept.

"Please forgive me," I said. "You know I wasn't the one who was talking to you that night in April—it was the devil, he had possessed me, he was in my evil thoughts, my voice, and he was trying to hurt you. I've been suffering too, and I'm still suffering. We're all going to get out of here, hang on, your wife and son are waiting for you, you mustn't disappoint them. Here, take this medicine, and you have to eat. Remember how we were friends in school, Lhoucine, and how we stuck together in Kenitra and even here, we're all in the same boat. You have to hold on—please, don't go, I couldn't stand it if you left us, it's so simple, we've almost made it! Do you see what I see? Come on, please, open your eyes, just look at this: your mother, your wife, and your son are bringing you a bowl of incense, preparing to welcome you. They've whitewashed the house. Everyone is expecting you. I'd like to go with you, to that party—tell me, you're inviting me, right? Afterward, we'll go to Mecca together, I swear I'll take you with me, just say yes and I'll invite you, we'll take the plane and we'll stop over in Cairo, we'll go visit the pyramids, I'll take you along to the café where Naguib Mahfouz goes, the Egyptian writer who won the Nobel Prize, we'll have pictures taken with him, then we'll go on the pilgrimage in style. No more exhaustion, no more hardship. Don't give up . . ."

He struggled to wipe away his tears and managed to say, "It's true, I can't be my son's father. I'm sure of it. You're right."

"No, absolutely not, you're wrong! That was just to hurt

you. I didn't really believe it. Lhoucine, please, I'm begging you, forgive me! I invented that story because you were attacking me. Your son truly is your son. He's waiting for you. Don't disappoint him. You have to get out of here, and you'll see, then this won't matter to you at all . . ."

I began weeping again. Lhoucine died in my arms. I held him tighter and tighter as I recited the Koran. Realizing that Lhoucine was dead, the Ustad joined his strong voice to mine.

31

Sometimes, like Camus's character, I thought that *"if I had been locked up . . . no . . . compelled to live in a hollow tree trunk . . . a hundred-year-old tree, the one where Moha lives . . . with nothing to do but look at the flower of the sky over my head, I would gradually have grown used to it . . . I would have watched the ballet that the sparrows . . ."* No . . . it's something with birds, clouds, and neckties* . . . I'm getting everything mixed up. But I know that my flower of the sky can only be Tebebt, my childhood bird, while the hollow tree is a block of clammy stone, and a ton of sand and cement to wipe out all memory of the sky.

I felt that a return to faith was more necessary than ever. After prayers, I meditated. I had been very distressed by Lhoucine's death. I dreamed about him: I saw him in a meadow, happy, with several children around him and his wife by his side. He was eating red apples. When I awoke, I wondered what it meant. A happy dead man—it could only be me, so mortified by guilt that I would give my life to have Lhoucine forgive me. I put myself in the hands of my guardian angels, whom I had decided to call Ali and Alili. Through prayer, I summoned them and conversed with them.

"If you are here, it's because God does not want to abandon me. As long as you are present, I will know that I am not defeated." They were there, silent. I called upon Allah and Mohammed. I recited all the names of God I knew. I repeated them, emphasizing the Merciful, the Compassionate, the Wise, and the All-Highest. I kept my voice low. Achar did not like to hear me murmuring. He thought I was plotting against him. He used to ask me what I was saying, interrupting my invocations. I would raise my voice to make him understand that he was disturbing me. He would begin praying as well, but since he was not very familiar with the words, he had to stop and ask for help. Fortunately, the Ustad would intervene and correct his recitation.

I was deep in prayer when M'Fadel banged on my cell door with his club. It wasn't mealtime. He opened the door and tossed me a box containing two sheets of pills. Opening Achar's door, he told him, "Here's a sheet of pills to take for pain. Don't forget this! I'm saving your life."

"Why did you give some to *him?*" asked Achar peevishly.

"Because he deserves it, you idiot!"

"Yes, but I was the one who asked you for them a long time ago."

"So what? If you keep griping, I'll take them away from you."

"No, don't, I was just asking, that's all . . ."

That was the day I wished I could pound Achar to a pulp.

The guards had opened all the cells and were allowing us a few minutes to see one another in the gloom by the faint ray of light filtering in from the entrance. For some unknown reason, Achar pounced on Wakrine, showering him with blows and insults.

"Son of a whore, you think you're going to get out of it like that, I'm going to kill you, I'll kill you!"

We all tried to separate them. Without even asking any questions, M'Fadel shut Achar up in his cell. For two months, every Friday, M'Fadel allowed us a short half-hour in the corridor but did not open Achar's cell. So there were no more incidents.

One day, Achar spoke to me humbly.

"Listen, will you take me to Mecca? I've so many sins to wash away, to be forgiven for. You won't let me down, will you? Hey, please, don't refuse me this favor, I'm so bad, so ignorant and jealous."

"I know you. If we get out, the first thing you'll do will be to go off to the whores. So stop filling this black hole with your stinking ignorance. Stop blaspheming!"

"It's true, what you're saying. You really do know me. I'm sure my wife's waiting for me. By the time I'm free, she'll be all wrinkled. I swear, if I get out alive—and I will get out of here—I'll marry a sweet young thing from my village."

"That's great, an innocent girl who'll be younger than your youngest child!"

"So what? That's life!"

"Achar, I don't want to talk to you anymore, you disgust me."

Having to put up with someone like Achar was exhausting. His interruption had disturbed my meditation exercise; the angels were not answering my call anymore, I no longer felt their presence. Over time, mental and physical wear and tear had taken their toll: all these trials had seriously impaired my ability to concentrate. I was having more and more trouble reaching my spiritual world. It was not that I lacked the will . . . I was worn out. Even today, I suffer the aftereffects of that ordeal. It's hard for me to read and write. I cannot concentrate more than a few minutes at a time.

I had to stop feeling anger at Achar or anyone else. Instead of obsessing about Achar, I moved on to the others. My father was first in line. I saw him in a silk djellaba, perfumed like a woman, jolly, pink-cheeked, smoothly shaven, impressively plump, with a mincing step and the bearing of someone always ready to bow to the king, eyes downcast and tongue quick to launch a witty remark at just the right moment to induce a smile—or even better, a laugh—from his boss.

I saw him and I grinned: how could I be angry at someone who was a jester at court and in life? A father who did not even remember that he had a family! He was not a melancholy clown. There was nothing tragic about him. He was all self-satisfied thoughtlessness, all passion for court and royalty.

I saw him and let him pass like a shadow through my life. It would have been easier to hate him, resent him, and nurse a need for vengeance. But that easiness was a trap: you begin by opening yourself to hatred, which then fatally poisons your blood.

After my father I saw silhouettes, the phantoms of those who had dragged us into that botched coup d'état. They were not all dead. There were still a few officers who had managed to save their skins through some fancy footwork. I did not hate them, either. They were perfect bastards. I had no enemies. I was not giving in to my worst impulses anymore. I understood how draining it was to spend my time chopping into pieces those who had done me so much harm. I had decided not to bother, and that is how I got rid of them, which amounted to killing them without dirtying my hands or stewing forever in the desire to repay them with the same misery they had inflicted on me.

I had to move beyond that idea of revenge once and for all, become impervious to its torments, because revenge smelled strongly of death and did not solve any problems. Search as I might, I found no one to detest. This meant I had returned to a state of mind I loved above all others: I was a free man.

32

Leaving aside the hypothesis of leaks organized by the authorities for political reasons, I kept wondering why M'Fadel, the head guard, the oldest and most cynical of the lot, would agree to carry messages to the outside, risking his life and the lives of his subordinates. Greed! He earned a great deal of money doing things for Wakrine. We had nothing left to lose. We had been in that death trap, watched over by the same guards, for more than seventeen years. People fall into habits, and we had ours. Only death came along now and then to interrupt this rhythm of survival. M'Fadel took advantage of all this. And we went through Wakrine to send as much information as possible outside. We took few precautions. We had no way of knowing what was happening out there. The main thing was to obtain some medications. And in any case, there was no way we could have much of a future. It existed by default: for some it was like a long death agony; for others, like a life frozen into little nothings where the fact of swallowing any medicine at all was the highlight of the year. We were counting on dumb luck to see some miracle happen in that hole, where there were fewer and fewer of us. We had no calendar anymore. Without a word of warning, our talking clock had given up the ghost. Abdelkrim, whom we called Karim, died in silence, of weariness and malnutrition. He had lost his appetite. A bad sign, the beginning of the end. Well before his final decline, he had asked me to take over his job. Which I did, performing much less well than he had. I was not in good shape, either. Sometimes I got the days mixed up. I was helped out by Fellah, Number 14, a noncom who had been sick when he began his imprisonment and whose health had remained poor. We split the work: he counted the hours, I did the days and months. Fellah was a quiet man, short and lean, and he claimed to have been poisoned by a woman.

"I'm *meouakal.* * She had me eat a honey cake in which her powerful sorcerer had put the most subtle of poisons: it doesn't kill but brings on every kind of disease."

"You're sure you're not just sick because of our imprisonment?"

"Here illness comes on naturally. But I'm pissing blood, sometimes with pus, and it's been nineteen years since I used my dick that way! So how do you explain that?"

I had come to think of Fellah as a kind of scientific experiment: attacked on all sides, his body fought back. He asked me for medicine.

"What kind?"

"Doesn't matter. I hurt everywhere."

Wakrine slipped him drugs. He swallowed them straight down. When we were in Kenitra and had access to the prison hospital, he used to ask for Valium. He took so much of it, I figured he was trying to kill himself. Not at all. He was already bewitched by that woman and was resisting through the Valium. At Tazmamart he was deprived of his tranquilizers. I thought he would go into withdrawal, but he adjusted, and if he was suffering, he didn't talk about it. He considered his imprisonment to be part of the "sorcery" campaign.

"That woman," he told me, "she swore she would make me pay. She succeeded. Don't trust the women of Kh'nifra! They are the meanest. She wanted me to marry her. Can you believe that? A whore picked me out for a husband! The mistake I made was going to see her a lot, on almost every leave. I had my routine. I'd get there early in the evening, she'd be alone with me, would fix me tea, then she'd get out a bottle of whiskey and we'd drink. We'd make love before supper. While I ate, she'd make herself scarce. I didn't pay any attention to that detail . . . We'd make love again a few times during the night. When I'd get out money to pay her, she'd become angry and kick me. One day she told me she wasn't seeing other men anymore, that I was her man, her chosen one. She'd left the big house where she

lived with other whores and had taken a smaller place. It was
out of the question for me to marry a prostitute! Can you imagine? The shame, the disgrace! I should never have gone back
there. But it just didn't occur to me—no such luck. Anyway, I
was already in trouble, she'd crammed me full of stuff that
makes you sick. I saw a sorcerer in El Hajeb, he was the one
who told me all this. To get better I had to consult several doctors besides the sorcerer, who was supposed to counteract what
the other one had prescribed. Only a sorcerer can remove a
spell cast by another sorcerer. I ran out of time. We left Ahermemou to go on maneuvers, and here we are."

"Wait a minute—you mean the coup d'état?"

"What coup d'état? We left early in the morning to go to
Bouzneka for maneuvers . . ."

"But you do know why we're here, right?"

"Yes, we've all been bewitched."

"Fellah, you're joking!"

"Me? Not a bit! One of the things I can't do anymore is
laugh and make jokes. After she made me swallow that stuff, I
lost the ability to laugh. Well, have you seen me laughing since
then?"

"No, that's true. Anyway, who feels like laughing in this
hole?"

I realized that Fellah was gravely ill. Syphilis drives you insane. He had kept his memory but did not understand what
was happening to him. I immediately lost all faith in his timekeeping and began counting the hours myself. His madness was
not obvious. He would be speaking coherently, then suddenly
say something incomprehensible.

"I remember Khdeja quite well. I'm obsessed by her. She had
huge breasts. I love that. She had very black eyes and two dim-
ples on her cheeks when she laughed. And then the horse
climbed up onto the minaret. He pissed on the people passing
by there. Yes, the general punished the fig tree. He took all its
figs and gave them to Khdeja. By the way, the general is the fa-

ther of her first daughter, the one who opened the door for me when I left to go on maneuvers. I remember clearly that morning when the neighbor lady's dog bit the Habousses' boy Nadir on the calf. He cried, I laughed. Khdeja gave me things to eat and to smoke. I must have smoked dried herbs from India or China. They were real strong. I didn't know where I was or what I was doing. That's what witchcraft is. I'm not crazy. Hey, don't you believe that I'm crazy. I'm sick. I have every disease there is, but I'll be cured by the end of maneuvers. Here, it's good, what we do. We're learning to resist cold, heat, scorpions, and cockroaches. But if the general would give me some medicine, that would be nice. It seems he watches us through Japanese binoculars. He sees in the dark. He gives everyone grades. Me, I'll never get good grades, because Khdeja refused to sleep with him. He'll get his revenge. A general is important. He can do anything. Nobody can say no to him, except Khdeja. I like her spirit, even if she did hurt me. When we get out, I'm going to go see her and tell her two things. First: bravo for not sleeping with the general. Second: what you did to me was not right! I'm sure she'll be sorry, because my penis is ruined. It's no use for anything now. When I pee it hurts horribly. I'll say all that to her. But you, you know so many things, tell me, when are maneuvers going to be over?"

"Soon, Fellah, very soon."

"You'll go with me to Kh'nifra to see the beautiful Khdeja?"

"Of course I'll go with you. I'll tell her that what she did was not right."

"You, you're my friend. Say, what time is it?"

"But you're in charge of the clock!"

"Oh, I forgot! But what clock do you mean?"

"The one here in the dungeon."

"Ah, you mean the clock in our barracks! That's been out of order for a long time. I have to fix it. In civilian life, I was a clock- and watchmaker. I joined the army to repair the generals' wristwatches. Have you noticed that generals are always late?

That's because they wear watches with lots of gold. Gold does not get along with time. You're better off with a watch of plain metal—that guarantees precision. My father taught me that, a long time ago. In the army they assigned me to general duty, although I wanted to work with time. I tried to tell them, but they didn't take me seriously. So, do you think I did right not to marry Khdeja?"

"Yes, Fellah, that was the right decision."

"When you go off on maneuvers, you can't leave a woman behind, especially not one like Khdeja. You might be wounded. I think I was wounded. I must have taken a bullet in the belly or my genitals."

"It's possible. You know, those were real bullets."

"Oh, I certainly remember that. The day before, the commandant was laughing when he told us, 'Maneuvers with live ammunition!' When he said it again, we all laughed. But you remember the French doctor who came over to the group of officers and said jokingly, 'What are you planning, a coup d'état?' And the captain told him, 'No, important maneuvers.' "

"Yes, I remember very well. You see, I'm not the only one mentioning a coup d'état."

"Yes, but we didn't carry one out. We haven't the balls for that. On the subject of balls, I'm fucked. Mine are useless now. Khdeja bit them, she swallowed up all my breath, my soul, my life."

"When we get out of here, when maneuvers are over, we'll go see Hadji Brahim, the most expert *fqih*, to counteract the effects of the witchcraft. You'll see, Fellah, everything will turn back against Khdeja. It'll be her turn to go crazy."

"Oh yes, my friend, we have to make her swallow hyena brains. I know an old Saharawi who sells them in Marrakech. If I screw her, she'll be sick for the rest of her life."

"But then she'll make everyone she screws after you sick, too, and that's not fair. You mustn't do that."

"You're right. I'd like some fish!"

Fellah spent the night clamoring for fish. He swore in Arabic and then in French. He knew an impressive number of words that mixed sex with religion.

That very night, I heard the funeral song of the screech owl, and thought, "Fellah's hour of deliverance has come."

No: it was Abdullah—a lieutenant and instructor, as I was—who died, after several weeks of diarrhea. He never told us about it. Day after day, his life had run out of him. He sat in it, lay in it. Foul odors no longer alerted us to the illnesses now living permanently in our midst.

Death has a smell. A mixture of brackish water, vinegar, and pus. It's sharp, astringent. The screech owl's cry was always accompanied by that very particular odor. We did not have to verify it—we knew it instinctively. In the morning, when the guards brought coffee, we would tell them, "Could be someone's dead. Better check."

Fellah could not pee anymore. He died after excruciating agony. He no longer spoke, but muttered, stammered, shouted, kicked the door, and then, after a long night . . . silence. Surprisingly, the screech owl had not predicted his death. There was no mournful song.

33

In my carefree days, I had a high opinion of myself. I was in a hurry. Life seemed beautifully clear to me. And happiness, too.

I was wrong. The only way to have a high opinion of yourself is through the esteem of others. To learn that, you must travel across several deserts and through several nights. I had resigned myself to enduring our ordeal without complaint. I never reproached anyone but myself, in the silence between two prayers. I prayed to God without thinking of what might happen or what those prayers might bring me. I expected nothing from them. Thanks to prayer, I was reaching the best part of myself with the humility of someone who is gradually leaving his body behind to escape the slavery of suffering, appetite, and delirium. My actions were entirely gratuitous, unlike those representing a calculated accountability established with God and His prophets. Believing in God, praising His mercy, saying His name, glorifying His spirituality— all that was a natural necessity for me and I expected nothing in return, absolutely nothing. I had reached a state of renunciation and inner ascesis that greatly comforted me. I, who had previously maintained that a person never changes, had become someone else. I was confronted with a different self, freed from all the fetters of the superficial life, needing nothing, demanding no indulgence. I was naked, and that was my victory.

After Lhoucine's death, after the crudely wounding things we had said to each other, I had understood that I had to take myself in hand again and return to the endless path of higher thought, invoking the most mysterious and secret Spirit, which surely dwelled in a universe to which I already possessed the keys, and the signs.

The black stone, the heart of the universe, the memory of

grace, the splendor of faith, and complete unselfishness: such were the signs that guided me. I should add the intermittent presence of my guardian angels, of Tebebt, and—alas—of the screech owl as well, our announcer of imminent misfortune.

I prayed quietly, letting myself be carried away by an inner music attuned to the occasion. I would no longer hear what the others were saying. The pains in my back and spine would continue plowing their furrows. Since I had begun to lose my powers of concentration, I took the medicines M'Fadel occasionally gave me. I managed, thanks to prayer and the recitation of Sufi poems, to reduce the intensity of the pain and sometimes even to leave behind this body that was battered and deformed, but still defiant.

Toward the end, my body no longer obeyed me. Now *it* was leaving *me*. So I tried to hang on to it, falling asleep curled up like a cat, clinging to the earth to keep my body from abandoning me entirely. I stopped thinking. I no longer imagined anything. I was empty. I had become an aberration in this hole that had already swallowed up fifteen of my twenty-two companions from Ahermemou. There is a limit to everything. My mind had just about given up.

It was now almost eighteen years since I had seen myself in a mirror. What or whom did I look like? When I managed to raise my arm, I passed my hand slowly across my face. Like a blind man, I used my fingers to see. My cheeks were hollow, the cheekbones hard and prominent, and my eyes had sunk deep into their sockets. I was gaunt.

The need to look at yourself in a mirror, to adjust some little thing or simply to recognize yourself, to confirm that it is indeed the same person—that lost and forgotten habit no longer interested me. What was the point of seeing yourself? In order to love others, it seems, you must have some love for yourself, but me—I had no one to love or hate.

One day, taking advantage of a thin shaft of light in the corridor, the Ustad asked me if his face was still in the right place.

Sensing my puzzlement, he added, "I mean, is my face on backward? Is my Adam's apple at the back of my neck?"

"Feel your face with your hand and see for yourself."

"No, I can't. My hand is numb."

He had lost his sense of touch but could still feel pain.

"I'm suffering inside," he told me. "My heart and chest are in a vise of anguish. I'm beginning to have doubts. I read the holy Book, I invoke God and our Prophet, may God's grace be upon him, and then I find myself back where I started, alone and abandoned. I dive into the ocean of the Book, a boundless ocean, I'm tossed about and I almost drown in the waves of words that all go in different directions now. My guts hurt, my head aches, and I don't know what to do. I'm telling you this today because I can't see any way out. I'm going to die without ever seeing the sun or light again. Perhaps, on the other side, hell will be less cruel than what they're putting us through here. I believe God will forgive me. God is justice. God is goodness. God is mercy. God is compassion. I long to be called to Him. 'And it is to Him that you will return.' I'm old, and I have hardly lived. That is my fate. I feel that my hour is coming. Please, don't let them cover me with quicklime! I'm counting on you to see that I go to God clean, in a white shroud, and that the prayer is said over my body. I'm going to recite now to remove this pain from my chest—it's like a bar of iron that weighs a ton, here, on my rib cage."

He had entered what we call *sukârat al-maout,* the rapture— or rather, the intoxication—of the dying. This intoxication is characteristic of the very pious.

His heart gave out a few moments later. We were still in the corridor. The guards did not move. The Ustad collapsed. I took him in my arms. He had time to raise his index finger and make his profession of faith. I held his hand and repeated after him the words every Muslim must say on leaving this world here below.

M'Fadel allowed us to bury Ustad Gharbi properly. There

were not many of us left. A guard brought me a white sheet to use as a shroud. It was the only burial performed with due ceremony. That day, the sky was gray, with a soft light. We stayed at the graveside for a little while, reciting the Koran. One of the guards wiped away a tear. We were all moved. We missed the Ustad's voice. I threw his rags down near the grave. As we turned to go back to the hole, Wakrine told me to look to the left. What I saw did not shock me but panicked the others: seven graves had been dug in the courtyard. There were seven of us left. They were our graves. On the opposite side, there were a dozen open graves. They had to be for the prisoners in the other cell block.

That evening the discussion was all about that sinister discovery. Wakrine, who was the most frightened, kept saying that he was going to fight, that he would never be taken to the execution post without a struggle. We all thought the same thing, but I was convinced that those graves were not for us. It was just a feeling I had. But how could I convince the others? I did not even want to try.

"A bullet in the back of the head."

That was Wakrine's obsession. He repeated those words in every possible tone and inflection; he said them in French, in Arabic, in Tamazight.

"A bullllet in the heeeaaad."

"*Kartassa felkfa.*"

"*Tadouat aguenso takoja'at.*"

"*Kartassa in the takoja'at.*"

Kartassa, a bullet, *tadouat, kartassa, tadouat,* a bullet, *kartassa,* the back of the head, the back of the head, *kartassa* . . .

Those words were driving me out of my skull. We were all tired, depressed, and profoundly disturbed by the Ustad's death. I calmed down and somehow managed to block out Wakrine's voice.

The next morning, I heard my Tebebt singing in a staccato manner, telling me about activity in the courtyard. M'Fadel arrived soon afterward and asked me how the night had gone. I was astonished! Not one of the guards had ever shown the slightest concern about our nights or days. He asked Wakrine the same question. It was Achar who answered for him.

"He kept us awake, he raved all night long. You mustn't wake him—he could start up again! 'Bullet in the back of the head, *kartassa* . . .' "

M'Fadel told him to be quiet, then opened Wakrine's door to find the prisoner huddled at the far end of his cell. Terrified, Wakrine clutched at the guard's right leg.

"Tell me you're not going to do that? Not you, you wouldn't kill me, right? My friend, my cousin, they're not for us, those graves, you're not going to put a bullet in the back of my head. No, not you. We know each other too well. We've known each other for almost eighteen years now. Tell the guy behind you to go away, tell him you're in charge here, please, get rid of him, he's threatening me with his automatic pistol! I've never seen that guy before, where does he come from? Who sent him? He's our killer—why isn't he wearing a uniform? He's from the political police? Do something, M'Fadel, those guys are dangerous! If he kills us, he'll kill you too, because you know too much!"

"Stop it, Wakrine!" shouted M'Fadel. "I'm alone. There's no one behind me. You're delirious! No one has come to kill you. It's me, your friend, and I'm here to ask you what you'd like to eat today. Do you want fish or meat?"

"Oh, I was right! It's the condemned man's last meal . . . You have to die with a full stomach, in good health, that's it—they pay attention before they send you off into the great beyond. Listen to me, guys, I'm not crazy! It's not normal for them to change our everlasting menu and ask us so nicely what we want! Hey, Brains, what do you think?"

"Me," I replied, "I don't think it's normal either. If they're improving our chow, it's because they're up to something. What? I have no idea."

"Oh, I do. Still, it's weird: the freshly dug graves, the burial of our friend the Ustad in the proper Muslim way, and then offering better grub. There's something tricky going on."

"Listen, Wakrine, control yourself and stop yelling. I'm sure even M'Fadel doesn't know what's in store for us. So quit shouting, say your prayers, and wait."

M'Fadel shut the doors and left without a word.

I thought about the Ustad and the huge emptiness he had left behind him. I could still hear his deep, glowing voice . . . He had not feared death and had never rebelled against our fate. He always said he was in "the pure service of God," that he was there to pray, not to pass judgment on his fellow men. One day he told me that man is more noble dead than alive, because in returning to the earth he becomes earth, and nothing is nobler than the earth that entombs us, closes our eyes, and blossoms in a beautiful eternity.

34

It was June 1991. We had received no news of the country and the outside world. I calculated how much time had passed between the first letter smuggled out of the dungeon and the slight improvement in our food. I made a connection between these two events, without thinking about hope—let alone any kind of victory. Five years of letters, of messages in bottles. How could I have known about everything being done by Madame Christine, by my brother living in France, by Omar's sister the pharmacist, Wakrine's wife, and many, many others who were spreading the word about this hell of ours that had been kept secret for fifteen years?

Wakrine had calmed down. But two other companions, Number 11, Mohammed, and Number 17, Icho, a Berber from Tagounite, were dying after long illnesses that made them cough until they choked. They needed specialized treatment. The rest of us took all the medicines M'Fadel brought because we knew they could only help us, given our general condition. Hearing those two cough, M'Fadel told me that we might soon be seen by some doctors.

"Who are those graves for?" I replied.

"How would I know? Stop asking me that kind of question. It's been eighteen years! You should have figured out that I'm just a guard in a very unusual prison. We've spent enough time together not to try and outsmart one another."

"Okay. But go see how Wakrine is. I'm worried about him."

M'Fadel spoke to him in Tamazight. Wakrine sang a lullaby from his childhood, and we went back to our survival routine. I thought about mirrors again, and about my face; it had lost all expression, or rather, had stiffened into a single grimace, that of a man who was annoyed and upset but not wondering why he had no more face. No matter how much I touched it, I was convinced my face had been stolen. The one I was wearing was not mine, not the face my mother used to caress . . . Besides, if by some miracle I were to meet my mother, she would not recognize me. It would take her a while to come over and hug me, the way she always did when I returned from a trip. And I was on a trip, after all: I was going around the world underground, gallivanting about the planet, crossing seas and mountains, bent over in a cell shaped like a grave on wheels and pushed by a drunken commandant. Bizarre animals encountered during this voyage tried to bite the commandant and set me free. I had seen a dead man cackling in a coffin carried by dwarfs; when he tried to sit up, the date halves set in place of his eyes fell out of their sockets. Now he was blind for good.

I saw an ailing stork lie down in the middle of the road and raise its wing to stop the wind.

I was hurled by lightning onto the curve of time, where I rolled head over heels. Instead of the drunken commandant, I now saw a long-tailed monkey smiling at me. Where was I? Why did I feel as though I were hitting my forehead against an immense window? I searched for a shadow where I could hide—I who was deprived of light!—but the shadow was cast by an oak and I was free to play with the grass, to twiddle my thumbs and catch a few butterflies. The dwarfs dropped the dead-man-who-wasn't-dead and came over to tie up my hands and feet without a word. One of them smiled at me. They all had M'Fadel's face. I laughed and crouched at the far end of my cell.

When I awoke the next morning, my head felt light. I was as cheerful as if I were returning from a wonderful voyage.

I had become the guardian of silence, refusing to negotiate with the long night of hope. I had to live through this night without avoiding its pitfalls, without clinging to stones, without eating the damp earth crawling with worms.

I learned that one could get used to anything, even to living without a face, or sex, or hope. I did not try to find out how the others were coping with their sex drives; I had solved my problem three days after I landed in the hole. Having decided that I had no more family, or fiancée, or past, I was no longer thinking about the outside world, and so did not allow myself to have any desires or fantasies. I used my penis only to urinate. The rest of the time, it was cold, reduced to its simplest form, and I was not even troubled by erotic dreams. My penis didn't protest, didn't stir, and didn't bother me. I never thought about it at all anymore. When poor Rushdie had complained about becoming impotent, I changed the subject. I was not afraid of dealing with the question of sexuality in prison, but felt it was each person's private concern. The fight against the invasion of life, against thoughts of the outside world, had to be relentless. We could not let anything happen or let anything we had left behind filter in: not dreams, or plans, or the perfume of a rose, or the scent of a woman. Our struggle was to raise and reinforce this barrier, even though the walls imprisoning us seemed covered with a special material that made them completely impervious. That is why we stopped insisting on going outside to bury our dead. At first we had snatched a provision of light, a little piece of sky, a bit of life—even if it was somewhat damaged by military brutality. That was before our struggle became radical. The day of Gharbi's funeral, I had often found myself closing my eyes. Even though it was gray, the sky was hurting me. Light did not interest me anymore. I thought that my victory should begin in the dungeon, or else I would waste away like most of my companions and die without ever fighting back.

The open graves no longer frightened Wakrine. It was he who woke me one morning, quite pleased to have found an explanation.

"You know, they dug them to scare us. Did you notice that after years of refusing they didn't hesitate to let us bury the Ustad? They knew that one of us was going to die. So they dug those graves to terrify us. You know, it's like when there's a fake execution. I saw that in an American movie. They blindfold the victim, the firing squad arrives, they give the order to shoot, the guns go off, and the victim shits with fear. The bullets are blanks. So are the graves! But we—we know we're not going to be in those holes dug in the courtyard. Anyway, the barracks courtyard isn't a cemetery. See, I've figured out their game, I'm not stupid, and you're not either, you agree with me, right?"

"Of course I do. They're pretend graves. Because if Rabat's orders are to liquidate us, they're not going to tire themselves out burying us each in his own spot. They'll throw us into a common grave and be done with us!"

"You're right. What are we doing today?"

"We're going to pray that our companions Mohammed and Icho don't suffer."

They died quietly, one week apart.

35

I no longer remembered which poet had said, "Death does not put an end to life." That idea haunted me, however, and I did not know how to explore it and share it with the few companions I had left in that summer of 1991.

There were only five survivors in Cell Block B: Achar, Abbass, Omar, Wakrine, and I. Death was still in the neighborhood, and what's more, in a hurry to get the job done. I had the feeling something was going to happen. Wakrine told me that, according to M'Fadel, razors and shaving cream had been distributed to the prisoners in Cell Block A. This sounded plausible. The prisoners in the other cell block often received better treatment than we did, perhaps because they had two or three important officers over there. In any case, I really didn't care about the rumor and refused to discuss it with the others. But it might have been a sign. Something was happening. Our distress signals must have been picked up by someone somewhere— maybe the foreign press was talking about us, maybe influential political figures were pressuring the authorities in Rabat, maybe intellectuals had mobilized to obtain our freedom, maybe even Jean-Paul Sartre and Simone de Beauvoir had intervened on our behalf and a petition was circulating in the offices of major newspapers. How were we to know? We had no idea what was happening in the world, which might well take an interest in our fate one day . . . I could not have known at the time that Sartre and de Beauvoir were dead; to me, the world continued to live in an unchanging little eternity. Perhaps they were going to shave us, wash us, give us decent clothes, and even move us to different quarters, to show us to Amnesty International?

They would put us in a clean prison, in cells furnished with beds, nightstands, electric lamps, new blankets, and they would feed us lamb, broiled chicken, and even fresh fish . . .

At the beginning of July, we were treated to some meat: for the first time in eighteen years, they served us camel meat, with potatoes and peas. The portions were generous, but the food stank: I had forgotten the smell of meat. I had not missed it. When I was little, I used to eat chopped camel steak at my grandfather's house. The meat had a particular odor, quite strong, and it nauseated me.

Distrustful, cautious, I ate only the vegetables and some bread dipped in the sauce. Poor Abbass gobbled down the fatty meat without chewing it and wound up with indigestion and a high fever. Instead of fasting, the next day he ate some beans and noodles. He spent an entire week vomiting, still with a high fever. He died at the end of July. Achar, who had eaten the meat, suffered no ill effects. He was still big and strong. Wakrine told me the meat was wormy and they were trying to poison us. Omar had followed my advice and did not touch it. Our stomachs could not digest food that was now so unfamiliar.

After Abbass died, they served no more meat, but they varied the vegetables, and instead of the evening noodles, we would have rice with tomato sauce.

For almost a month, my little sparrow, my Tebebt, my Lfqéra, sang a melody that was both lovely and sad, a song that gave me the feeling there would soon be a departure: his, mine, ours—I did not know. I gave him some rice. He was being treated to an improved menu, too. The screech owl was gone. The prison had lost most of its occupants. Something had to happen. The four of us speculated, each in his own corner. I kept track of the time. Omar was confident, convinced that our messages had had an effect. Wakrine fell prey once again to the anguish of uncertainty. Achar made plans for when he got out, while I tried not to think about the future. At night I dreamed that I botched my release: everyone would leave the prison, forgetting about me; I would be asleep, and no one would think to wake me. Or else the Kmandar would call us together, give a speech, and just when he was setting us free, he would detain me, saying, "You, you're staying here. Your father intervened to prevent your release. You'll remain alone in the prison until you die." At that point I would wake up sweating, cursing the night and slumber that had spawned that dream. One morning I recited the Kmandar's speech. I could remember every word.

"*Balkoum!* Attention! *Raha!* At ease! I am your comman- dant. My name is Debbah, the butcher. I have always been a man without feelings, either good or bad. I serve my country, my God, and my king. You were twenty-three strong when you arrived in this prison. There are only four left. So you see, my mission has not been 100 percent successful. As God is my wit- ness, I have done my duty with discipline, integrity, and strict adherence to orders. But, well, here you are: proof that every- thing is in the hands of God. For you, it's over, or almost. You are pardoned, that's all. There's no particular reason for this. It isn't Independence Day, or Mouloud,* or Aïd Kébir.* You will return to your cells. You will be given horses and you will go. Attention! Dismissed!"

That was when he called me over to say that I had not been pardoned.

Achar thought that this dream was meant for him.

"Actually," he told me, "you don't want to see us get out. The way I interpret your dream, it's that you want us to stay here while you're the one who leaves, because your father has arranged to have you freed. I've always heard that a dream means the opposite of what happens in it. Which doesn't sur- prise me, you selfish bourgeois pig!"

I was careful not to let him provoke me. My dream was sim- ple: after eighteen years, my father felt guilty. With age, faith gives way to fear, or else faith conceals fear. My father had to be afraid of God. He knew that he had behaved badly toward me through egotism, cowardice, and the need to please his king.

I recited the Koran by myself. Wakrine complained of pains in his joints. He was having more and more trouble moving. Omar was counting to infinity. As for Achar, he dreamed aloud of what he would do when he got out.

"Me, it's not complicated, I've always been simple and straightforward. When I go home, I'll sell the house and buy a delicatessen in Marrakech. I'll stock things imported from Europe. I'll get married again, the way I already told you, and I'll make a new life. If my wife and children got along without me for twenty years, they can keep on doing it. I've forgotten them. I had to. Time passes. What was once dear to your eyes and heart fades away. My first day out, I'm going to eat in a real restaurant. I'll get drunk, I'll go piss in the cemeteries. Ah! I've got to stop, because I don't know if I can make it until our release!"

He had no doubts and not one scruple. My dreams were chaotic, and my doubts were legion. I was a seasoned prisoner without any illusions. Achar no longer got on my nerves. Omar's counting mania did not bother me.

That night, I fought my last battle. It lasted for hours. Death had its claws in my heart, trying to tear it out, while I was pulling in the opposite direction to hold on to life. I was just not going to let death get the better of me after eighteen years in that dungeon. I knew I would win. I was sweating. I could see death's angry face gritting his teeth and sputtering with rage. I refused to give in, never doubted I would win. After one last all-out effort, calling on every ounce of my meager strength, I felt the claws let go. As if punched full in the chest, I collapsed, exhausted but with a sense of peace and even well-being that I will never forget. I was alone with my aches and pains, my thoughts, and a body in such wretched shape I could not even have donated it to science. I was weary and alone. I could feel my vertebrae all jammed together, my stiff fingers, my twisted shoulder, hunched back, empty body, and my tangled thoughts suspended in some neutral space, neither black nor white, at the end of something . . . In life I would have said I was at the end of my tether, but here I found it hard

to imagine what our tether would look like. Probably a hang-
man's rope.

The day I told my companions the story of Buñuel's film *The
Exterminating Angel,* my companions shouted in terror. I
Moroccanized the film script and told them that the famous
dinner took place in a superb villa in the wealthy neighborhood of Anfa in Casablanca. We happened to be there, setting the table and providing security for the officers and their
wives. We were in the garden under a tent while the Moroccan
haute bourgeoisie—businessmen, politicians, society women—
stuffed themselves with every imaginable delicacy. And then, at
the last stroke of midnight, an invisible window came down
from the sky, imprisoning them, leaving them to fight among
themselves in their attempts to escape from that house of misfortune, a glass house of cruel fate for people who no longer
knew who they were or with whom they were living. We
watched them and had a few beers. They saw us laughing and
called for help, cursing and raving. We couldn't do a thing for
them. The glass was unbreakable. It was the will of God, divine
justice, and we, thrilled and uneasy, had no idea how this
drama would end. A miniature civil war was unfolding before
us. They were ripping one another's eyes out, battling with the
cutlery from this elegant dinner party. Blood flowed, and tears;
there were women with their breasts falling out of torn dresses
and their buttocks exposed, and their men were biting one another. They had become monsters, cannibals, revealing their
true nature. Then a flock of sheep came down from the Atlas
Mountains and surrounded the house, grazing the lawn. The
colonel's wife danced drunkenly while another woman had her
gold belt and diamond necklaces pulled off. How could anyone
not laugh at this hideous spectacle? Behind the tent were gathered all the servants who had felt compelled to leave the house
without knowing why; now they said that it was God's justice,

the Last Judgment. When the glass barrier was lifted as dawn was breaking, and the guests began adjusting their clothing, we were kind enough to take our leave and not watch their humiliation to the bitter end.

Why did this film obsess me? Why had I put it in a Moroccan setting so real it became believable? A beautiful story, a miracle of intelligence. That is what we missed and needed most: intelligence.

At the end of my story, I asked Buñuel to forgive me for having set his film in my country.

As usual, Achar had not understood the metaphor of the invisible barrier, or the abulia that had afflicted those fashionable society people. He had protested, demanding a logical explanation.

I thought of this film on that day when my courage and perseverance failed me, and I imagined the Kmandar stalking into our hole, flinging open the cell doors himself, telling us, "Get the fuck out of here! You're free . . ."

We would go toward the exit, and there an invisible spiderweb, spun by the devil or the Kmandar's orderly, would prevent us from leaving. We would turn and face the astonished Kmandar. His eyes glittering with hatred, he would burst out laughing, and without even shutting the cell doors, he would leave us alone with our catastrophe.

36

How could we have known that we were living the final months of our martyrdom? M'Fadel had changed his attitude and would come talk with me in the corridor. He said some peculiar things, and while I listened, nodding my head from time to time, my thoughts were elsewhere.

"You know, you—I like you. You're not going to believe me, but if you guys leave here, you're the one I'll miss the most. What do you want—I'm only human. I'm used to you. I admit it was real tough. In fact, at the beginning, I didn't think your bunch would last very long. I thought—we all did—that none of you would make it through one year. Human beings are amazing! They have unsuspected reserves of willpower. They resist in spite of every obstacle. I know, not all of them did. But you realize—if you get out, you'll be a walking miracle! Guess what, we even took bets on who would die when. Your lot did something intolerable and you've paid for it. Rules of the game. Imagine, if the coup d'état had succeeded, today we'd be fellow officers in the same barracks. I'd even be your subordinate. At fifty-eight years old, I'm only a noncom. You, by now you'd be a commandant or a colonel. Life is strange. Here, I brought you more vitamins, take them, they can't hurt you. I went into a drugstore and asked for some vitamins. A young woman gave me this box, the pills are supposed to contain all the daily requirements."

"And me, I just die?" yelled Achar.

M'Fadel had forgotten about him.

"You, you'll never croak, not with your fat pig's belly . . ."

"But I hurt, I've got pains all over. Please, give me some medicine!"

M'Fadel let him grumble and left, shutting the cell doors as he went.

In that instant I experienced a moment of great peace. Nothing more could happen to me. Go, stay, survive, die . . . It was all the same to me. As long as I had the strength to pray and to commune with the Supreme Being, I was saved. I had finally reached the threshold of eternity, which men's hatred, their pettiness, and their meanness would never touch. I had thus attained, or so I thought, a sublime solitude that lifted me above the darkness and beyond the reach of those who preyed on the helpless. Nothing in me moaned anymore; my limbs had been reduced to silence, to a form of immobility somewhere between repose and death.

I had come to the limit of resistance. My body had already ceased to obey me. My head was swollen from going over and over the same prayers, the same images. And yet . . . I knew that soon we would be flooded with light. I was preparing myself by closing my eyes and imagining this reunion. I was giving in a little to this temptation. I was no hero, but a man who had managed, in spite of eighteen years of tribulation in that dungeon, to cling to his humanity, in other words, his weaknesses, his feelings, and his ability to confront seismic forces he had for a long time refused to acknowledge. My fortress was crumbling. I heard the voices of those who had left us. It was all whirling together in my head, which I could no longer hold in my hands. Vanquished by pain and sorrow, I had lost the protection of my solitude. I was not alone with my faith anymore. There were intruders in my inner domain: I had been invaded by evils. I refused to say the word "agony"— I preferred "madness." I climbed up on the capital M and stretched out my arms as if to dive into the blue water of a swimming pool. I clung to the firm roundness of the d. I fell off, and clambered back on. Grabbing the e, I looped it around myself and clutched it as though it were a life preserver. But what was happening to me did not correspond to the usual meaning of the word. Saved by the madness of nature, by the insanity of my imagination. "Madness! Madness!" I sang.

Luckily, nobody else could hear me; my voice hardly resembled one at all anymore. Other words came to my rescue. I was in an ocean of words, a shifting dictionary of flying pages. The most comfortable word was "astrolabe." I loved its pleasing sound, the song I sensed within it. Of course, that had nothing to do with the instrument that calculates the position of the stars. Although . . . Astro and Labe = aspire and labor . . .

After prayers, I was brought back to my cell by a harsh cry from Wakrine that echoed in the emptiness left by those already gone. It was like a long and powerful thunderclap in a black sky. Wakrine could not stop howling. His suffering was such that he did not know what he was doing. He had become uncontrollable; no longer in possession of himself, he seemed to be struggling in the jaws of a predator. When I spoke to him, he did not hear me. There was nothing to be done. Perhaps he had seen death and was refusing to give in?

Through all our dead companions during those eighteen years in the hole, I had become rather familiar with the angel Azrael, the one sent by God to gather the souls of the dying. I would see him, humble, dressed all in white, patient and soothing, trailing behind him a perfume from paradise that probably only I could smell, for it lasted a mere moment or two. I recognized his passage from the chill little wind that blew through the prison, and I knew he was gone when his fragrance filled my cell. A prettier image than death as a skeleton with a scythe.

That day, I detected neither his presence nor his scent. Wakrine would have to go on suffering. His hour had not yet come. By nightfall he had stopped shouting, but he cried like a child in a tumult of tears.

For breakfast we had fresh bread. It must have been baked two days earlier. The crumb was still soft. The coffee was the same as always: dromedary piss. But for the first time, they gave us some sugar. I had completely forgotten the taste of sweetness. I found it bitter. My saliva had lost the habit of this kind of food. Achar let out a hoot of satisfaction. He thought our release was imminent. Omar made no comment. As for Wakrine, he came slowly back to life, and ate the bread and the sugar.

At lunchtime they served us cans of sardines and an orange. For supper, the usual noodles. They did not want to spoil us too much all at once. It was July, and one of the guards had the effrontery to tell us, "Today is the festival of youth, the birthday of Sidna, whom God preserve and glorify . . ."

The next day, early in the morning, they came for Achar. He left his cell blindfolded and handcuffed. He thought he was going to be freed.

"Goodbye, friends," he said. "I'm the oldest. In Morocco, we've always been nice to older people. It's only natural that I be the first to get out. I suppose it won't be long before they let you go."

A guard ordered him to be quiet.

I heard later that he and an officer from the other cell block had been transferred back to the civil prison in Kenitra. They stayed there until a few months after our release.

That night, I had the following dream.

We are all wearing white shrouds and are gathered in a mosque. We pray without stopping. We are side by side but do not speak to one another. Between prayers, we perform the traditional bow. I have trouble walking, because the shroud is tightly wrapped around my legs and hands. When I pull on a string by my fingers, the cloth covering me falls to the ground. I am not naked: another shroud covers my body but does not hobble my feet. I can walk. I leave the mosque while my companions pray. No one notices my departure. Stepping outside, I am greeted by a burst of bright light. I close my eyes and see my mother. I keep walking, and nobody pays attention to me.

I did not dare think that the mosque was the prison or that the prison could be represented by a house of prayer.

37

One of the worst nights of my imprisonment was that of September 2, 1991.

We were all taken to Cell Block A, which had more survivors than we did. Omar, Wakrine, and I were in a frightening state of debilitation and fatigue of both body and spirit. We had trouble walking and staying on our feet. Wakrine was crawling, while Omar had to lean against a wall to keep from falling down. M'Fadel came over, gave me his arm, and said, "Hold on to me. It's the end of the nightmare. I think it's the end. I don't know any more about it than you do, but all this seems like something coming to a close."

I nodded; I hadn't the heart to speak.

We were barefoot. They had blindfolded and handcuffed us. A voice we did not recognize called the roll. That's how I learned who had died in the other cell block. Twenty-eight survivors out of fifty-eight convicts. Thirty tortured, thirty dead, thirty martyrdoms of variable duration and ferocity.

They put us in trucks. I heard the canvas flap fall and seal off the back of the vehicle. Our bodies were roughly shaken all night long, as if the road had been chosen specifically for its wretched condition. The trucks drove on side roads, even on dirt paths.

I felt our truck slow down. Other military vehicles arrived from the opposite direction. I gathered, from conversation between our two drivers, that these vehicles were bulldozers, not trucks full of convict soldiers who would be taking our places.

"Boldozer, ya boldozer!" exclaimed our driver to his assistant. "It's iron—iron that eats everything, uh-oh!"

"We have to let them by, or they'll squash us."

"You're right—you can't argue with iron!"

I could not think anymore. I imagined. I invented. I saw

metal jaws hanging from giant cranes, and then bulldozers coming to destroy everything. No more prison, no more hole. The dungeon torn apart, its walls demolished, the stones reduced to rubble and sand. Those voracious machines would go all over, crushing every building. I spared a thought for the scorpions: they would become dust and sand as well. But why destroy everything? Ah—to eliminate all traces of that horror! Even worse than the experience of horror is the denial of its existence.

I flatten you, break your back, shove you into a pit, I let you die by inches in utter, lifeless darkness, and then I deny everything. It never existed. What? A dungeon in Tazmamart? Who is this insolent idiot who dares think our country has committed such a crime, such an unspeakable evil? Throw him out! Ah, it's a woman! Well, what's the difference, get rid of her, she'll never set foot on Moroccan soil again! Traitor! Pervert! Barbarian! She dares suspect us of having organized a system of slow death in complete isolation! What gall! She's the tool of our country's enemies, who envy our stability and prosperity. Human rights? But they are respected—just look around you! Political prisoners? No, we don't have those here. The "disappeared"? The police are searching for them. We have to give the police credit, because they do a wonderful job.

This speech ran and reran through my aching head. I smiled. So, they were going to demolish our dungeon. I imagined soldiers attacking slabs of cement, getting all sweaty and out of breath. They would be forbidden to speak or ask questions. "Orders from headquarters." A secret operation. It would even have a name: Rose Petals, because of the *moussem* of Imelchil,* when men offer roses to the women they would like to marry. A delicate gesture. I pictured other soldiers transporting palm trees—freshly dug up from the palm groves of Marrakech— and trying to plant them right where men had experienced the ultimate in torment. But then I imagine—or even suspect and affirm—that the palms are reluctant. The soldiers plant them, try to anchor them, attach them with ropes, but the palms refuse to stand up, they lean and fall to the ground, raising a cloud of red and yellow dust. The soldiers choke, cough, then get back to work. It's no use. The palm trees will not accept this doubtful earth, this accursed place that has seen bloodshed and tears wept in vain. Palm trees do not grow in cemeteries. So the soldiers will take their palm trees away with them and go to the forest of Maamora to uproot a few oaks or beeches and try once more, with Operation Rose Petals, to camouflage this shame.

Even if the soldiers manage to erase all trace of the dungeon, they will never erase from our memories what we endured there. Ah, my memory, my friend, my treasure, my passion! We must hang on. We must not fail. I know—weariness, and so many troubles. Ah, my memory, my child who will bear these words across to the other side of life, beyond the visible! So go ahead: demolish, lie, camouflage, dance on men's ashes, you will grow dizzy and then there will be . . . nothingness.

Pain and fatigue silenced me. My head seethed like boiling water. My thoughts were dissolving: images eddied restlessly, then sank into the night. My shoulder hurt. My back hurt, my skin hurt, and even my hair ached. My neck and hands were stiff.

Our journey lasted a good twelve hours. When the trucks stopped, I thought for a moment that we had returned to the dungeon. We climbed out of the truck, and a soldier led us away. He took me into a room, removed my handcuffs and blindfold. When I opened my eyes, I had to close them because of the pain, and I waited, leaning against a wall, to understand where I was and what was happening to me. Slowly, I opened my eyes again. I immediately noticed a small window, high on the wall, letting in light. Despite my extreme exhaustion, I smiled for the first time in a very long while. The soldier told me that I could lie down on the bed. I remained where I was, as if I had not heard him. In a tone of mingled respect and compassion, he repeated, "Lieutenant, you would be more comfortable lying down." How did he know I was a lieutenant? It had been twenty years since anyone had addressed me like that. I remembered being promoted to that rank on July 9, 1971. The following day I was to have worn my second star. The soldier helped me to the bed. I lay down on my right side. The earth quaked, the bed shook from side to side. The walls pressed in on me, then drew back. I saw the ceiling glittering with tiny lights. I felt as if I were falling into the void. I landed on bags of wool or cotton. It reminded me of my first parachute jump, when I had felt a pang of fear in my heart. But this fright was much worse, as if my parachute were not opening. My body, so sore all over, was being sucked downward. I was cold. I felt weightless, and giddy. I had to get off this soft bed right away. My skin could not bear any softness. My body was a patchwork of all kinds of scars. My soul was intact and even stronger than before, but my skin had been too damaged. I tried to get up again. I clung to the mattress to keep from falling. After a few tries, I managed to stand up, hunched over as if I were still in my cell. The ceiling was high but seemed low to me. Pulling off the blanket and sheets, I lay down on the floor, which was cold and hard. That reassured me. I could finally sleep, dropping into the deepest of nights.

I was awakened by a different soldier bringing me a tray of food the likes of which I had not seen in a long time: half a broiled chicken, mashed potatoes, a tomato and onion salad, fresh bread, and best of all, a pot of yogurt. I looked and looked at this meal without daring to touch it. Then I ate the bread, potatoes, and yogurt. I thought I should wait a few hours before starting on the rest. When I did put a piece of chicken breast in my mouth, I had trouble chewing it because half my teeth had fallen out and the rest were loose.

When I swallowed, I felt nothing. The food had no taste. Next I ate the tomato slices and drank a large glass of water.

That evening, they brought me another tray just as richly laden. It was a feast. I drank the vegetable soup and ate the ground meat. My stomach began hurting immediately. I should not have eaten so much.

That night I tried again to sleep on the bed. It was just too comfortable for me. I spent another night on the floor. In the morning, a doctor came to see me. He asked me questions of a strictly medical nature. I replied without comment. I showed him where I hurt. He examined me for at least an hour. He ordered blood and urine tests for me and prescribed medications for me to take.

Three days later, I saw a different doctor. He must have been some kind of specialist, and he was concerned about my gall bladder.

"You need an operation. Not right away, however, because given the state you're in, you wouldn't survive. Take these pills in case of an attack and we'll see about the operation later . . ."

Other doctors paraded through my room. I must have been an exceptional case, a phenomenon, since I had survived the vilest mistreatment. My body bore witness to that.

After two weeks in this gilded cage, a medical orderly took me to a dentist, who had arrived with a trailer equipped with all the necessary apparatus.

The vehicle was parked just outside the corridor of the building where my room was. Looking out the window, I recognized the place. The trees had not changed, or the mountains, either. The sky was a curious color.

To take care of us before they set us free, they had brought us back to the Military Academy, from which we had left to launch the coup d'état twenty years before. We were in Ahermemou, transformed into a recovery clinic for the survivors of Tazmamart.

That day will remain a historic event in my life: as I sat down in the dentist's chair, I caught sight of someone above me. Who was that stranger peering down at me? I saw a face suspended from the ceiling. He was mimicking my every expression. He was making fun of me. But who was it? I almost screamed, but I controlled myself. That kind of hallucination was common in the dungeon. But I was no longer imprisoned. I had to bow to the unwelcome evidence: that face—worn, creased, furrowed with wrinkles and mystery, frightened and frightening—was my own. For the first time in eighteen years, I was looking at my reflection. I closed my eyes. I was afraid. Afraid of my haggard eyes. Afraid of the haunted look of a man who has narrowly escaped death. Afraid of a face that had aged and lost its semblance of humanity.

The dentist himself was shaken.

"Would you like me to cover the mirror?" he asked kindly.

"No, thank you. I'll have to get used to this face I've been wearing without knowing how it was changing."

He was shocked by the state of my teeth, I could see it in his stunned expression. A considerate and tactful man, he would have liked to sympathize with me, but changed his mind when he saw how oddly I was looking at him. Was he frightened of me, of my terrifying appearance, or was he so upset by my general state that he just could not say a word? He sighed deeply, placed a mask over his nose and mouth, and tried to remove the tartar from my teeth. Blood poured from my gums. He stopped and told me, "The next time I'll do a gingivectomy." He gave me some pills to take and helped me stand up. As I walked along, I looked for that other face that had taunted me. The soldier accompanying me said, "Don't worry, lieutenant. No one is following us!"

We had a barber who kept our skulls and chins shaved clean. One day I asked him to get me a mirror.

"It's against orders," he replied. "We're supposed to take care of you here, and they're afraid you might get some crazy ideas."

"All right. I understand. But could you at least let me see my face in your mirror?"

"I haven't got one."

At the end of a month, I began to resemble a normal human being. I just had this one problem: the look in my eyes unnerved everyone who saw me.

The psychiatrist pretended not to be disturbed by my eyes. He asked me questions, which I answered briefly.

"How do you feel about the army?"

"I don't feel anything."

"Any resentment, desire for revenge?"

"No."

"What do you think of your family?"

"Family's family."

"What do you think of your father?"

"He's someone who loves his children, but he isn't a father."

"Do you resent him?"

"No, not at all."

"What will you do when you leave here?"

"No idea. Perhaps take care of my health."

"I've been told you had a shock when you saw your reflection in the dentist's mirror. Is that true?"

"Yes, it's true. My eyes looked like those of a madman, although I haven't lost my mind. There was also death in my eyes, yet I am alive. I have not accepted having those eyes, there's something frightful in them. They're the eyes of a lunatic. I'm afraid. And I see fear in the eyes of others. Maybe I should have prepared myself for that shock. I'll get used to it, in the end."

"You will, I'm sure of it. Have you been dreaming since you arrived here?"

"Yes, I dream a lot. Even back there, I dreamed all the time. They weren't all nightmares."

"Can you tell me about one of them?"

"From now or before?"

"Let's say, a dream that had a powerful effect on you."

"This is a dream I often had. I'm in Marrakech, in an old house in the medina. It's a *riad** with patios and large rooms. In the kitchen, I see my mother. She doesn't see me. I walk by and head for the room in back, where there's a well. It's covered with a cloth my sisters embroidered when they were in school. I'm in this dark room. I see two men digging a grave to the right of the well. The earth is piled up to one side. Shining little snakes come out of it. They don't scare me. I haven't any voice or willpower, I'm just there. The two men grab me by the arms and throw me into the hole they've dug. They push the dirt back in on top of me, very quickly. I don't move. I don't try to cry out. I'm buried but I see and hear everything going on in the kitchen. I see my mother preparing a meal. I see the maid washing the floor, I see the cat chasing a mouse. I'm not afraid. I don't feel anything. I laugh all by myself, and no one comes to get me out of there. Well, that's it, doctor. I love this dream because it shows how I really felt. I knew I wasn't going to die in Tazmamart."

"Thank you for your cooperation. I have nothing to add to what you've already said. May God keep you!"

38

After two months of medical care at Ahermemou, we learned we were going to be released. The authorities would choose two or three prisoners to be sent home, and hand them over to the police in their respective districts. We never knew until the last moment who was getting out and who would have to wait.

My turn came two weeks after the first group had been released. I was in my room when the Kmandar appeared, accompanied by a doctor.

"Sidna the king has pardoned you. In a few days, you'll be rejoining your family. You will certainly be contacted by foreign journalists, by people who want to harm our country. There is clearly only one way to deal with them: do not answer their poisonous questions. Do not collaborate with them. Refuse to have anything to do with them. If you try to make trouble, I will personally drag you back to Tazmamart! Understand?"

I had decided to remain silent, to refuse to play their game. But I could not let this pass.

"Listen, Kmandar Debbah, take back that last part, because nothing could be worse than Tazmamart!"

"How do you know my name?"

I had managed to surprise him.

"You look suspiciously like someone I knew at the Military Academy. So keep your threats to yourself. And I have a request."

"A request? What do you mean?"

"If I leave here, it will have to be lying down. I'll need a mattress. Otherwise, I'll be arriving home on all fours, and I suppose that wouldn't look too good for the army, the police, and even the country."

"Doctor," asked the Kmandar, "would you say his condition is as bad as he claims?"

"Not only is he in extremely poor shape, but he must travel lying down, or I cannot guarantee that he will reach Marrakech alive."

"All right. You'll have a mattress."

He left, then returned and asked me through the half-open door, "What year were you in the academy?"

"What difference does that make? We're not going to sit around reminiscing about old times!"

He slammed the door, and that was the last I saw of him.

They came to get me the next day—in the middle of the night. They brought me a suit, shirt, tie, and shoes, none of which were my size. I left dressed in a jogging outfit.

The trip lasted almost twenty hours. I was lying down in the back of a truck. The bumpy ride was excruciating and seemed to take forever. We reached Marrakech that evening. I heard the call to prayer, car horns, motorcycle noise . . . the music of life.

I was dropped off at the headquarters of the Royal Police Force in Marrakech. They were expecting me. I was taken to an office and led to a chair placed in the center of the room, where I sat facing a row of seated police officials. I crossed my arms and stared at the caid who was speaking to me. You would have thought I was being court-martialed.

"Sidna the king, may God protect and glorify him, has pardoned you. Tomorrow you will rejoin your family. But be careful, foreigners will certainly contact you . . . ," and so on.

He spoke solemnly, arrogantly, and all I heard were intestinal rumblings, farts, the gnashing of teeth, the amplified sounds of a deranged body. His face was changing shape and especially size; his drooping lower lip touched the desk, where his hands were playing with a ruler. His teeth dropped out with the clatter of falling stones. His nose was running. He was dripping with sweat. The caid was oblivious to all this, continuing to threaten me while I kept staring at him. The more I stared, the more he stammered, tripped up, repeated himself while trying to find the right words. The mere look in my eyes was paralyzing him. He struck the table with a ruler, sending the pages of a dossier flying around the room. At that point, beside himself, he began shouting.

"Lower your eyes! You're before the caid, the superintendent of police, the precinct captain . . . So, I was saying, if anyone contacts you, you'll let us know. Agreed?"

I did not say a word. I just kept staring at him. He started fidgeting, lit a cigarette, began tapping on the table again.

"That's enough!" the superintendent told him. "Leave him alone!"

As I left the office, I recognized my younger brother with a young woman. I simply stood there, looking at them. His eyes brimming with tears, my brother threw his arms around me and said, "Do you recognize Nadia? She's your little sister!"

Nadia was crying, while my eyes were empty. At home I had trouble recognizing my two little brothers. They had been nine and eleven years old when I was arrested. I asked to see our mother. She was in El Jadida, under medical care. As I had long feared, she was seriously ill. In my grief I did not say anything. I felt dizzy. I could not fall asleep. I lay down on the floor, under the table. I curled up like a wounded animal. I changed position, got up, banged my head against the low table and fell back onto the carpet, stunned, completely lost.

It was October 29, 1991. I had just been born.

39

My birth was another ordeal. I looked like a little old man who had only recently come into the world. I had shrunk by five and a half inches and now carried a hump on my back. My rib cage was deformed, my lung capacity diminished. My hair had held up well, but my skin was crêpey. I dragged my right leg when I walked. The words I spoke had been winnowed: I chose them with care. I was close-mouthed, but my mind was constantly at work. I was a newborn who had to shed his past. I decided not to remember anymore. For twenty years I had not lived, and the man who had existed before July 10, 1971, was dead and buried somewhere on a mountain or a verdant plain.

How could I make those around me understand that I was a whole new being, somewhat travel-worn, who had no connection to the person they expected, the one they had seen go off one day and not return? Words were not enough and misled those who took them literally. So I refrained from speaking, from commenting on things, from participating in social life. I heard them talking about me.

"He's still in shock."

"He's weird!"

"That's what it is, he's traumatized. And who wouldn't be . . ."

People wanted to invite me, to organize parties, to honor me, to give me presents. Some tried to make me talk about that hell. They thought they were pleasing me. They could not understand how far away I was, clinging to my prayers, in exile in my world of faith, spirituality, and renunciation. I slept on my stomach, with my arms outstretched, like an unknown man abandoned by a roadside. I was afraid to lie on my back. I was a stranger lost in a world where I recognized nothing and no one.

After five months, I was still having trouble with the ease and comfort of my new life. When I entered the bathroom, I would admire the faucets for a long time. I would look at them and not dare use them. I stroked them as if they were sacred objects. I turned them delicately, and when water came out, I used it sparingly. I paid attention to everything. It was hard for me to get used to slippers. I walked on tiptoe as though I were afraid of falling or of dirtying the marble floor. My hearing had become particularly acute. Nothing escaped me. It was irritating. Sounds were growing louder and louder. In the silence, the buzzing in my ears became constant and shrill. My eyes absorbed images indiscriminately without even identifying them. I was like a sponge. I filled myself with whatever came within reach, snapping it all up. I understood from this that I was a newborn of a rare kind: I had just come into the world and was already full-grown. Everything astonished me, enchanted me. I stopped trying to comprehend it all, and I simply gave up trying to explain the state I was in to my family.

To sleep, I needed a hard bed. I had a plank put underneath my mattress.

Doctors considered my case. They could not figure out how I had managed to survive. I needed silence, and solitude. Difficult to find in a family that was rather more boisterous than most.

I preferred to go sit next to my mother. She had cancer, but she suffered without a murmur.

"I would never dare complain in front of you," she told me. "I know, my son, what you endured. No need to tell me about it. I know what men are capable of when they decide to hurt their fellow men. I am content to have seen you—I was so afraid of dying with this wound in my heart. My life is now in God's hands. If He calls me to Him, so be it. No tears, no wailing; simply a few prayers and kind thoughts. Tell me, my son: I hear that you have seen your father! How did that come about? And how did it go?"

"It was the simplest thing in the world. At your granddaughter's twentieth birthday party there were musicians, a *chikhat,** and lots of friends. I was invited. I did not want to stay too long at this kind of gathering. Father arrived late, as usual. He made his entrance like a king. He had his young wife with him; she seems like a nice person. He was dressed in silk and smelled of a woman's perfume. When he took a seat, I got up and went over to him. I bent down and kissed his right hand, the way I have always done. He asked me how I was. I told him I was well. He said, 'God bless you.' I left him there, surrounded by his entourage, and returned to my place. As if nothing had happened, he told for the umpteenth time the story about the Algerian hairdresser who refused to pay rent for his house to Pasha El Glaoui."

"You know, my son, he has never been a father for any of his children. He loves them, but you must not ask too much of him. He has always been like that. Sometimes I called him the Honored Guest. You mustn't hold it against him. Tell me . . . It seems that Tazmamart never existed?"

"So they say. It doesn't matter. It's true, it never existed. I have no desire to go see for myself. Apparently, a small forest of old oak trees has moved over there to cover the huge pit. They even say the village is going to change its name. They say . . . They say . . . ."

GLOSSARY

Ahmed Chawqui: B. 1868; d. 1932. An Egyptian poet and play-wright who introduced modern themes into classical Arabic poetry.

Aïd Kébir: The celebration of "the slaughtering of the lamb."

babouche: A Turkish or oriental slipper.

Ben Brahim: El Houari Mohammed Ben Brahim Assarraj (also known as Cha'ir al Hamra) was born in 1893 and died in obscurity in 1954. Beloved by Moroccans as "the Poet of Marrakech," and befriended by his illustrious patron, Thami El Glaoui, pasha of Marrakech, this *poète maudit* was an irreverent iconoclast and an acerbic critic of the established moral order.

chikhat: A group of female singers, accompanied by a violinist and a tambourine player, hired to perform popular songs.

couscous: A North African dish of granulated flour steamed over broth or meat. "Seven-vegetable couscous" is a dish made in the spring, with lima beans, zucchini, carrots, turnips, bell peppers, onions, and chickpeas.

djellaba: A loose-fitting hooded robe worn by men in North Africa.

djinns: In Islamic mythology, a class of spirits lower than angels, capable of assuming human or animal form and influencing mankind for good or evil.

esparto grass: A tough, wiry rush of Northern Africa, also called Spanish grass, used to make cordage, paper, shoes, and other articles.

Fatiha: The first sura, or chapter, of the Koran ("the Recital"):

IN THE NAME OF GOD
THE COMPASSIONATE

THE MERCIFUL
Praise be to God, Lord of the Universe,
The Compassionate, the Merciful,
Sovereign of the Day of Judgment!
You alone we worship, and to You alone we turn for help.
Guide us to the straight path,
The path of those whom You have favored,
Not of those who have incurred Your wrath,
Nor of those who have gone astray.

King Hassan II is said to have ended the massacre at Skhirate by reciting the Fatiha when confronted by one of the leaders of the revolt.

fqih: Originally, someone who teaches the Koran; by extension, a scholar. From his knowledge of the Koran, he may act as an exorcist. (The *fqih* Hadji Brahim bears the honorific indicating he has completed the hadj, the pilgrimage to Mecca every Muslim should make at least once in his or her lifetime, during the month-long period of Ramadan.)

gandoura: Lighter than the djellaba, the gandoura is an ample, almost sleeveless robe that sometimes serves as an undergarment in East Africa.

Green March: The area now called Western Sahara was a protectorate of Spain in 1957 when a rebel movement ousted the Spanish, who with French help regained control of the region and made it an overseas province of Spain. In the early 1970s, dissident inhabitants formed organizations seeking independence, including the Popular Front for the Liberation of Saguia el Hamra and Rio de Oro (Polisario). In 1975, the International Court of Justice rejected Morocco's and Mauritania's claims on Spanish Sahara and upheld the right of the native Saharawi people to self-determination. Hassan II of Morocco, however, had already organized the Green March (named after the holy color of Islam): more than 300,000 Moroccans (some volunteers, some not) massed to invade Spanish Sahara. The Saharawis appealed to Spain to defend them, the United Nations dithered, and Moroccan troops clashed with Polisario guerillas in the northeast of the disputed territory. On November 5, Hassan ordered the marchers across the border. With 160,000 Moroccans already inside the territory, and a growing danger of war between Morocco and Algeria (which supported Polisario), Spain finally agreed to negotiate directly with Morocco. The Madrid Agreement left the southern third of the territory to Mauritania and the rest to Morocco, which has administered the entire area since Mauritania's withdrawal in August 1979. The UN does not recognize this annexation, but the Moroccan monarchy uses the issue to foster national unity and pride, so the status quo continues.

Imelchil: A gathering at which men buy peasant girls, some of them as young as twelve, as brides.

Jamaa El Fna ("Mosque of Desolation"): Once a place of execution, this vast square at the heart of Marrakech is now an open-air market and arena for festivals, street performers, fortune-tellers, dancers, musicians, and hustlers of all kinds.

Kaaba ("square building"): A cubical shrine in the courtyard of the Great Mosque at Mecca containing a sacred black stone (said to have been given to Abraham by the archangel Gabriel), the chief object of Muslim pilgrimages, toward which believers face when praying.

kelb/kleb: *Cleb,* French slang for "dog," is derived from the Arabic for "dog," which is *kelb* in the singular, *kleb* in the plural.

medina: The native quarter or "old city" of a town, not to be confused with the holy city of Medina, in Saudi Arabia, the site of Mohammed's tomb.

meouakal: Said of a submissive husband, whose wife is assumed to be doctoring his food with mysterious substances to control his behavior.

Mouloud: The celebration of the birth of the Prophet.

neckties: Arrested for the murder of an Arab, Meursault sits in jail and reflects that in time one gets used to anything: "I've often thought that if I had been compelled to live in a hollow tree trunk, with nothing to do but look at the flower of the sky over my head, I would gradually have grown used to it. I'd have watched for flights of birds or drifting clouds, the way I now kept an eye out for my lawyer's outlandish ties, just as I had once waited patiently, in another world, to make love with Marie on Saturdays."

Oufkir: General Mohammed Oufkir, the second most important man in Morocco, tried to seize power in 1972 by having King Hassan II's plane shot down. After the failed coup, Oufkir was liquidated and his wife and six children—one of whom was only three years old—were imprisoned. In 1987 several of his children escaped and managed to contact French journalists before being rearrested. The family was finally freed in 1991.

riad: A traditional villa, typically a large, airy house of several stories centered on a garden courtyard with a well or fountain.

Sidna: A term of respect that can mean "King" but may also mean simply "Sir." "N'am Sidna" would be "Yes, Majesty."

Skhirate: A suburb of Rabat, the capital of Morocco. For most of the first half of the twentieth century, Morocco was a French protectorate; following a period of political turmoil, Morocco became independent in 1956, and Hassan II became king in 1961. In July 1971, over a thousand soldiers stormed the palace in Skhirate, killing almost a hundred guests at the king's forty-second birthday party. One year after this abortive coup, there was another assassination attempt when Moroccan Air Force jets attacked the king's plane in the air. Unrest continued, but the king maintained relative order through a policy of suppression. Hassan II, who died in 1999, was a passionate golfer, and left his impoverished country well supplied with beautiful golf courses.

souk: A bazaar, a traditional marketplace or shopping quarter in the Middle East.

Sura of the Cow: The suras of the Koran are generally arranged in order of length, with the longest first. After the exordium of the Fatiha comes "The Cow," a long discussion of precepts of the faith. Its name comes from a brief reference to Moses, who tells his people that God commands them to sacrifice a cow. The people demand further particulars—what kind of cow? what color? etc.—but, in the end, "they slaughtered a cow, after they had nearly declined to do so."

Tamazight: The language spoken by Berbers, the original inhabitants of North Africa, and the Tuareg. The word "Berber" comes from the Latin *barbarus,* a person who did not belong to the Roman world, but the Berbers called themselves *Amazighen,* free men. In Francophone Arab countries, Berbers often feel that they and their language are the victims of discrimination.

tanjia marrakchie: A tajine is a stew cooked over a charcoal brazier in a shallow dish with a conical lid (this traditional clay pot is also called a tajine). The *tanjia marrakchie* ("in the style of Marrakech") is made of specific cuts of lamb that are seasoned with the Moroccan mixture of herbs and spices called *ras-al-hanout,* sealed with dough in a special cylindrical and very tall clay pot, and cooked overnight in a baker's oven.